UNKNOWN DESTINIES - VOLUME 1

Edited by Fiction4All

UNKNOWN DESTINIES – VOLUME 1

FICTION4ALL

TABLE OF CONTENTS

What Bot Invaders?
(Geoff Nelder)

Leanne's resumption of consciousness drove her dream ever faster into forgetfulness. Her eyes opened slowly, inviting the question why was it so light? Had they left the bedroom light on? Ye Gods, it was daylight and too much of it! She kicked the duvet off the bed.

"Jon, wake up, we've overslept. We have to get Amanda to school, her SATs start today."

He growled, scratched his nether regions, and reached for the cup of cold, half-drunk drinking chocolate. "Hey, Lee, you're the electrician, didn't you set that new alarm clock last night?"

She reached for her grass-green Sigma Electrics coverall. "I did and it's five to nine. You'll have to get her to school while I dash to work."

Outside she was still gargling mint Listerine because her Smaart toothbrush vibrated so fast her skull rattled and she had to abandon it. What was going on? Now her car door wouldn't open obliging her to use the manual key. "What the hell, Jon?" she yelled even though he should be inside the house, urging their daughter into her school uniform.

The stench of stale Doritos was bad enough but to leave such detritus on the driving seat... ugh. At least the hybrid's dashboard lit up and the engine hummed when she pressed the starter. Her relief didn't last more than a few seconds when the vehicle put itself into reverse. Luckily, the foot brake overrode the not-so Smaart e-car's autonomous controls before she made a hole in the garage door.

She tapped at the control screen to turn off all the computerised aspects of the drive although it wasn't possible to disengage every electronic or actuated component in a modern vehicle. At least she could drive the thing and get to work using one, mostly screaming gear.

Four miles later she pulled up at the building site, noting hers was the only car although several bicycles and a skateboard leant against the canteen wall.

Three men uniformly dressed in tan cowboy-boots, grey hoodies and blue jeans sat on a tatty, old sofa in the corner all leaning forward watching a TV. Leanne made herself a coffee and joined them.

"Hey, guys, any of you had trouble—"

Col, the foreman, interrupted her. "The whole world has, Lee. Electronics have gone berserk."

Nev, a Jamaican fitter, said, "Wife says it's the rise of the machines like Vernor Vinge says in his *Technological Singularity*, but she reads too much sci-fi. Makes her paranoid. I told her—"

"Strange though," Col butted in. "My own Smaart TV wouldn't come on at first and then it came on, off, on, off in sync with our electric fire. Too hot an' all. Neither would stop till I yanked the plugs out. I was glad to get out of there. Then me car wouldn't start. You're our leccy, Lee, what's going on. A massive solar flare? An Electromagnetic Pulse from a Ruski space station?"

Leanne sniffed at her Italian Rich Blend coffee then fished out a couple of strands of her auburn hair normally kept back by a band and hard hat. "Can't be an EMP, can it?"

"Why not?"

She pointed at the TV. "'Cos that's working— it's not steam-powered."

Colin scratched his head making Leanne wonder if that's why he was now bald. "Our Ring doorbell played up dead early, too. Kept ringing even though no one was there, then didn't ring when the postman tried it. Left a parcel to get wet on the doorstep."

Nev pointed at the TV showing an all-electric bus taking its passengers, screaming, into a canal with the driver running after it. "No one's going to trust any electrics after today, whatever's causing it. There, I'm taking off my new Fitbit before it decides to stop my heart beating instead of just measuring it. Oh my God, should I remove my mini-med insulin pump? It could kill me if it wanted to!"

They all looked at him. "Good point," Col said, "but can't you switch it off with an app?"

"But that's electronic too," Leanne said. "And it'll be the same for anything with programmable semiconductors. The new pacemakers, e-mood enhancers, cochlear implants, remote-controlled sex toys—oops."

"The list is endless but how is it happening?" Colin said, "The government will have to convene another Disaster Emergency Committee."

"And they'll take years and millions in expenses to come up with no answers," Nev said, pointing again at the box, this time showing a

9

robotic lawnmower chasing pensioners around a park.

Col stood, finished off his mug of coffee and coughed. "We'd better get on with this retirement complex before the project manager finds us gawping at TV."

Leanne stood too and walked to a bench where her tool belt waited. "Now then which tools can we trust not to turn on us?"

Nev laughed. I'm glad mine are just hammers, chisels and saws. Hang on, my drivers and drills are electric."

Fearing the worst, Leanne set to installing the latest heat pumps and boilers. Suppose whatever was causing the electronic malfunctions affected all the equipment she'd just fitted? As it happened, they appeared to be working properly via the remote sensor and app. The AI component she was reluctant to activate, worked beautifully, but she worried.

Back to the canteen for lunch. Peanut butter and sliced tomato sandwiches—her favourite, thank you, hubby Jon.

She wondered if the kettle would behave as it should and it did. Who wanted AI in kettles anyway? Some genius decided commuters would want their tea as soon as they arrived home so the kettle knew the time and so turned itself on if it had enough water. It knew—somehow—whether its owner wanted tea or coffee. Tea shouldn't be steeped above 85 degrees Celsius. Instant coffee to be at spot on 80, not boiling like your granny did them. The clever kettle would know which of its owners would be first through the door—from GPS location pinging their mobile phones—and reroute the heating, if necessary, to their barista coffee maker instead. She wondered if the machines could turn against their 'masters' overcook the beverages or learn how to make them toxic.

"Hey," Nev yelled and giggled simultaneously, "Everything's working now. Said on the radio. Must've been a glitch in the ether. Haha."

Um. Leanne knew of spikes and frequency faults that could make electronics misbehave but not globally and simultaneously.

Two weeks passed with no further problems at work or on the news. Leanne worried though that her career could shudder to a halt if it happened again and was astonished that Jon and the media didn't worry too.

Computer studies was her forte at college and it came in handy for her job. At home she pulled out one of the under-bed drawers, and dug out a laptop she'd not used for two years. No Windows on this baby. She plugged in a USB dongle before switching it on so that the Operating System booted up from it and displayed a closed Linux distro she and a few dark-web friends created a while ago for pirate apps.

She sent a private message to her former hacker friends.

'say Gan*g. Le& here. looking into the weird stuff on the 12th. anyone found oddities?'

While she waited for a reply, she hacked into the downloaded code of her own Smaart car that had gone wrong that day but was apparently fine now. The machine code filled the screen while she plugged in another monitor for her own programming. Out of habit, she had downloaded the original coding for the vehicle when she'd bought it, as she had for all her devices. She ran a subroutine to find any differences between the car system coding then and now.

There! In moments several lines blinked in red at her. While she frowned at the bizarre coding, a ping announced one of her hacking gang had sent a reply.

'hey Le&. you're slow, some of us isolated what seems to be corrupt lines last week. sending a screen dump of it. don't try and run the code, it might unhinge God-knows-what. Ka%'

"yeah, Ka%, i've been busy. some of us have proper jobs you know. same anomaly as in my Smaart e-car. not looked for it elsewhere. you?'

'everything we examined, so far. what you rekon? global glitch from a solar flare or like?'

'dunno. north koreans maybe? some of their red-star linux bots are similar.'

'it's like the kind of bots used in malware to infect computers and devices but Mik3 tried the code on an isolated laptop using a north korean OS and it fell flat—error messages galore. we were hoping you'd log in cos you've contacts at GCHQ ain't you? they must have solved this mystery and if they've not maybe they could use what we know to stop it happening again.'

Leanne had to think. Yes, a former boyfriend now worked at the radio section in Cheltenham but could she trust him to keep any contact anonymous?

'i do but maybe hold fire. we're a secret group. hell, we've not even met face-to-face. we have to ensure any message we send to my contact can't be traced back to us.'

'no probs. set up a false IP trail. we can make it look like it's come from the king. ha, I like that. anyhow, why can't you just phone him and tell him that you worked it out yourself. he knows you're sharper than razor wire, don't he?'

'but so's he. he's not much into coding but his colleagues have to be so they're bound to know what we do. leave it a while, Ka%. back in touch tomoz when i've done more searches.'

'just a mo, Le&, tune into al jezeera. fuck, its happening. reports of malfunction airplanes, not just kettles and cars this time and from countries that sat on it officially like russia and iran. think now we should send what we know to your pal before everyone in the world either goes mad?'

She deleted the errant code from the operating system but when she rebooted, it was back. Reinfected from other boot-up files. It would take a complete scan to find every instance of the bot code and delete them all before rebooting. If it was a normal hacker's bot she could write a patch to nullify it but it wasn't. She tried to do that, rebooted, and it was back. Grrr.

***

It took an hour before she sent a visual of their discovered bot—if that's what it was—to Steve, her ex: narcissistic, hunky, egoistic, charming, womanising, handsome, sickeningly-correct boyfriend and while insufferable, the only contact

13

she had at GCHQ. She didn't need to sign the message and she did the trick of rerouting it via numerous encrypted servers. Thing is, would Steve remember that she was into coding? It was while they were students. A lot of women and prosecco has passed under the bridge since then. He'd probably just pass it on to the relevant department. His speciality was installing listening posts on sensitive borders. Just as she pressed Send her lights went out. Could just be a fuse…

It wasn't. Every light in Clacton took a hike, maybe all of Essex, Britain, Earth. Although they all came back on an hour later. No explanation from the Energy Minister or anyone. Just light circuits were involved though. How was that possible? She chewed at a braid of her red hair while searching her brain for what smart tech was involved in domestic lighting? The consumer unit was new and did have a circuit board and was linked to AI-involved units in the house but not every residence had up-to-date equipment. The bot infections must be further up the distribution line even to the power stations, transmission lines, substations and smart voltage boosters.

Later that evening both of Leanne's smart televisions lost their screen images to a white blank screen for three minutes, followed by animated wavy black and white lines inducing reactions on social media and radio worldwide from annoyance and anger to epileptic seizures.

"With no TV and my phone on the blink, are we going to the pub or an early night?" Jon said while standing in the gloom of their lounge lit by a flickering screen and the orange street light streaking in through their first-floor flat window.

"You go, I need to try something."

"Lee, you're not downloading those bot things are you? Thought you'd left that life behind."

"Just to see if the corrupt code has changed since last time. I'll see you down the Horse in half an hour. Tops."

He opened the door. "I might be back if the pub can't pull any pints. They'd soon run out of bottles."

Leanne waved at him and continued on her laptop. It wasn't connected to the web and its non-standard operating system appeared to be immune from the bot infecting other devices. She'd taken apart her neighbour's drone that'd stopped working and downloaded its operating system onto a memory stick, now plugged into her laptop. The machine code appeared on screen. To most it'd look like random letters and numbers but to experienced programmers, certain patterns emerge. Again she ran a search subroutine and the anomalous code showed in red. Unchanged from the first cases. She was about to message Ka% when an almighty crash and a yell of, "Freeze!" made her jump.

She just managed to press F12, a key that triggered a macro that would wipe and burn her laptop's memory, including the dongle, before a taser sent her quivering, falling off her chair to the floor.

***

Leanne woke up with a massive headache and handcuffed to a table via a chain. She couldn't stop hot tears pouring down her cheeks. She had no idea how long she'd been unconscious, which police station she was in or how her ex had worked out it was her who'd sent him the message. Someone gave her tissues. The chain rattled as she dabbed her eyes.

Her main interrogator was a skinny man, way past middle-age, badly shaved and with spectacles he had to keep pushing up the bridge of his nose. The whiney voice of Superintendent Blunt had already dealt with his own and Leanne's identity and had swept aside her protestations of innocence.

He asked again, "Is your plan to drive everyone mad?"

"Is it working?"

"Thusly make us more vulnerable for an attack?"

"This is already an attack, isn't it?"

"A real, physical attack."

"You mean an invading force of a red army? Really?"

"You tell me, Miss Cazacu?"

She'd already explained that her husband was a Romanian but was now a UK citizen, a fireman helping to solve problems not make them.

"I should have kept my maiden name, Brown."

To her right, under a barred window, a hot and cold drinks dispenser suddenly gurgled and steam puffed out of the top.

The woman detective, a dead-ringer for Bjork, curled her lip and leaned forward, making Leanne tilt her own chair dangerously back.

"How come a jobbing electrician like you knows how to use machine code?"

16

"You have a laptop there. If you have a browser running, press the Ctrl key and U, go on. It won't do any harm. Try it."

Bjork had an intelligent look but clearly struggled with dancing eyebrows as to whether to Ctrl U or not. Her partner nodded. They'd have plenty of spares. It was a simple shortcut to view the source code on any Windows computer browser—usually. Harmless but impressive to those who'd not seen it. Bjork clearly had not. She stood up and back, knocking her chair over.

Leanne laughed. Good therapy for stress. "See, you're using code. Does that make you a Russian double agent?"

Just as the woman was righting her chair, the door opened, revealing a large man though more of a silhouette from Leanne's point of view. Larger was his voice.

"Out! All of you. Not you, Cazacu. Leave everything where it is!"

Superintendent Blunt stood and slammed Leanne's file on the table. "Why is MI5 so interested in our local hacker?"

Now he was closer, Leanne could see the Security Service investigator better. He wore a dark blue suit and his round face and bald head seemed too small for his body. He turned off the old-fashioned recorder that was taping her interview. Presumably, the iPad and CCTV recording wasn't reliable with the bot problem.

She was distracted by the drinks machine when a cup dropped into its place to receive a hot beverage even though no one in the room had

17

approached it. Leanne could quaff a cola no problem.

She was determined not to be beaten by these arrogant bureaucrats.

"I demand to see a lawyer."

"No need, you've not been charged…yet. Just assisting us with our enquiries."

He frowned at Bjork's laptop screen. "This is merely the source code for the page she was on—"

Leanne rattled her handcuff chain. "Don't turn it off. Let's see if even that simple page of code has the bot? I can give you the first characters to search for."

He had surprisingly jet-black eyebrows that he'd lowered to glare at her.

"It will be safe, Sir. Just three characters you wouldn't expect see in any page's source code. If that laptop has been turned on anytime within range of Wi-Fi, Bluetooth or Xender for example it's probably picked up the bot."

"How, exactly?"

Leanne's eyebrows went up in opposition to his going down. He must know the basics, surely?

"Really? Just like we shouldn't open or download suspicious files in emails or memory sticks then find bots harvesting our contacts or overwriting code as ransomware. You must know this?"

He coughed into his hand. "Of course, but how did you do that globally and instantane—"

The door opened yet again. "Stop this interview now!"

It was like a *Men in Black* convention.

18

Baldy stood and tried to puff himself even bigger, but the smaller moustachioed man merely said, "This is for us, comms and signals intelligence. Remove yourself and leave everything on the table." He flashed a lanyarded ID at baldy, who squinted at it.

"MI8? We do have a kindred interest."

"All right, but only as an observer."

They settled into their chairs and both stared at the laptop between them. Then looked to their left as the drinks machine beeped, probably indicating that the hot coffee, tea or chocolate was waiting. Everyone ignored it.

Moustache pulled at his nose. "Now Miss Cazacu, never mind the washing machines, Smaart cars and airplanes, how did you hack into our Storm Shadow cruise missiles?"

Leanne released a groan and hit the table with her forehead while muttering, "I didn't do anything. We—I only used a search routine to find the anomalous bots that might or might not have something to do with the malfunctions."

"You expect us to believe that? We tracked the message to your GCHQ contact, who is now in custody. It came from you and only you."

"Good grief. Wrong, wrong and more wrong. Let me show you. On that screen, merely the source code for whatever page is showing on the screen's left panel, do a search for the following three characters: tilde—"

"Stop right there, Missy."

"What? Nothing can happen. The bot I've found on everything I've so far seen is two-hundred and fifty-four characters long. The first three can't do anything and yet I've not seen code using them like that - ever. Give me a pen and I'll write it down."

Baldy hesitated but handed over a felt tip and started to rummage in his case for paper but before he'd found it, she'd drawn on the tabletop: ~ ʊ ϴ "There, tilde, upsilon and theta but search with no spaces. Do you need me to tell you the ASCII codes for them?"

Moustache shook his head. "I'll find them, but tell me what will happen."

"Do you agree that those three symbols are not normally found in source codes?"

He shrugged.

"When you run a search such as 'Find on this page' in the browser open on your computer it will find a chunk of two-hundred and fifty-four characters starting with those three."

As if bored of the humans, the drinks dispenser spluttered hot water over the floor. Baldy glared at Leanne as if it was her fault…a misbehaving bot in its works she'd planted there via an email.

She said, "Just unplug it from the wall."

He did but it continued to gurgle. Presumably, rechargeable batteries kept it alive.

Moustache tapped on a smaller device from his inside pocket. Leanne supposed he was finding the codes for the three symbols. Then he followed her instructions and glared at her.

"They're there. What does it mean?"

"How should I know. I didn't create that bot. I only found it. All I know is that it sits there on every device carrying code such as every AI and electronic device I tested."

He continued, "But it exists on this laptop, yet it is still working while other devices are failing even if only temporarily. How? Of course, there must be something in that bot's code that is waiting for a trigger, maybe sent to it from something else—"

"Yes, like a sensor running data at it," Leanne paused. "But these characters might only be odd because the originating signal couldn't find an exact match…" She closed her eyes while thinking.

"Miss Cozzie—"

"Cazacu."

"What are you saying by 'originating signal'?"

She rattled her chain in excitement. "Don't you see. Anything displayed on a screen can only show what it can pick from the operating system's database of symbols. Greek, Unicode hex, whatever. If the original signal was from a different device with a different symbols database, the bot might either just fail to insert itself or pick the nearest equivalent symbol. Depends on how it was programmed. The result is though, that we're all driven insane by our everyday devices, and now secret defence equipment failing at apparent random times. You know what this means don't you?"

Baldy looked at moustache and said, "The North Koreans or Chinese have sent these bots to unhinge us and disable defences to prepare for invasion?"

Leanne groaned again. "Can't be them, can it? Are their devices randomly disabled too?"

Baldy nodded.

She continued, "So, not from a country then, or at least not from humans. I presume you've considered a supersmart Artificial Intelligence has designed its own bots, or a network of AI doing the same to get rid of the pestilence of humans. If not AI…is anyone checking for anything unearthly hiding on the dark side of the Moon? It's aliens isn't it?"

At that moment the laptop fizzled, smoke rose making Leanne pinch her nose. Both the men hastily dived into their pockets to take out phones, fobs and other devices that were simultaneously bursting into flame. The light went out. The only illumination was from the drinks machine.

"Damn," Leanne muttered, looking at the dispenser unit, "They were listening."

The End…really.

Clickety Clackety
(Wynelda Ann Deaver)

"Clickety clackety, miserly wiserly" cried the old man. Jenna looked at him appraisingly; wondering what she had ever done to deserve this sort of attention.

He wasn't too bad, for a crazy old homeless beggar. A horn honked on the road, and Jenna shook her head. Not too bad? His old combat boots were missing enough leather to be considered sandals. His toes didn't just peek out of the boots, they fairly leapt out of them. His denim pants were stained beyond redemption, and his old pea coat was frayed at the hem and the cuffs. And his hair... the white mass stood on end as if he had been electrocuted. A normal crazy old homeless beggar. Only one oddity threw off the conclusion-- his hands were clean. Even under the nails.

Jenna took a deep breath and shuddered as she exhaled. Her nose wrinkled slightly, not sure if the scent were really there or if it was just the memory of an odor that was annoying her. Slightly woodsy, as if someone's essence was intertwined with that of a tree.

"Clickety clackety miserly wiserly," he cried again, his blue eyes pinning her in place.

Finally, a spark of recognition. Jenna sighed with relief. She had seen those eyes before-- their blazing, electric blue that made you feel as if you'd been burned. "If you wanted to fool me, then you really should have worn colored contacts."

"Damn it all, girl. How's a wee runt supposed to know a trick like that?" The man's appearance shifted, blurring until he stood in his true form.

Jenna looked surreptitiously to the left and right. Thankfully, they weren't in a conservative portion of the city. This area was known for its "artsy" flair, and the "wee runt" certainly had that. His combat boots had become soft, supple leather decidedly un-military in appearance. Soft butterscotch leather breeches were tucked into the boots, and a billowy white shirt tucked neatly into the waist. At least he wasn't wearing the large, plumed hat that he had been so attached to the last time she had seen him.

His features changed too, the lines of age and liquor smoothed out. Hair that had been an untamable white mass became soft, black waves that caressed his shoulders.

The only way that she could guess his identity were his smell and his eyes. They were the only things that always remained constant. And he was decidedly not a runt. He topped her by a good three inches, and she was five foot eight. If his kind considered him a wee little runt... then what were they really like?

"Well, you know the rules. You've got to guess my name. Guessing my name is your game. Clickety clackety miserly wiserly."

She had, in fact, almost exhausted the realm of known first names for this game of his. "Why, exactly, do I have to guess your name?"

"Because it's your game. The name's the game, and whoever wins..." His blue eyes clouded, troubled.

"Sins?" Jenna tried helpfully and was rewarded by the return of the mischievous gleam in his eyes.

They had played this game many times before, and it still puzzled her to no end. Why should she try and guess his name? And why in heaven's name did he try to rhyme so much? He wasn't even consistent about it for Pete's sake! A poet this man wasn't.

She racked her brain for a name she hadn't used already and came up blank. Always before she had tossed out the first name that came to mind. This time, though, felt different. "How long do I have to choose?"

Dark brows knitted, he looked at her warily. "Excuse me?"

"Is there a time frame for my choosing a name? Do I have to do it with in, say, ten minutes?"

He smiled slowly, and her heart twisted. A memory niggled at the back of her mind, but try as she might, she couldn't quite grasp it. It would be easier to try and spin straw into gold.

"I don't believe that there is a limit to the time we spend, although truth be told, lass, I've never asked."

"Would you like to go for some coffee?" She bit her lip, waiting.

"That sounds like just the thing, it does." He proffered his arm to her. It was such an archaic gesture, yet still she smiled as she placed her arm in the crook of his elbow.

The café they found was small and filled with chatter. They located, against the odds, a small table in the back, a little bit away from the crowd. She sipped her mocha, thoughtfully eyeing his coffee. Irish Crème.

Before she could think better of it, she reached across the table and took the cup from his hands. With a wicked grin, she took a gulp of his coffee. As the liquid hit the back of her throat, memory exploded in her soul.

The two of them trying to out-run a storm, laughing as they dripped water on the wooden floors of a cottage. Him, holding a steaming cup of coffee that she took out of his hands for the first sip.

"Who are you?" she cried.

"C'mon, lass, you know I canna tell you." His eyes were gentle, probing. "The name is the game you were called to play."

"Clickety clackety, miserly wiserly. Is there a meaning to that?" Jenna fought to control her breathing. She knew him, knew him beyond the times that she had met him on the street.

Her soul knew him.

"Aye. It has meaning." He reached across the table and reclaimed his coffee from her. His hand brushed hers in a casual caress.

It was more than she could bear. She stood abruptly, knocking her chair over. "The only name game I know of involved a little man named Rumplestiltskin."

"Is that your guess then?" His eyes bored into her.

They saw too much.

"Yes."

"Ach, lassie, we have but one more meeting. Until then…"

And he was gone.

Jenna found her way back to her apartment. It was small, but had never before felt cramped. Now, though, it was crowded with the images of a cottage set among a grove of trees.

***

She slept little in the weeks that followed, haunted by dreams of broken fairytales. Good kings turned bad by the lust of gold, women waiting for princes to come rescue them while layers of dust covered their coffins. The dreams were always silent except for an odd noise, muffled in the background. A noise she couldn't identify.

Always in the dreams there was a set of electric blue eyes that pierced her very soul.

Jenna wouldn't have noticed that she had lost weight, except for the fact that her clothes didn't fit properly any more. They hung on her worse than hand-me-downs. She looked this way and that in the mirror, but there was no hope for it. Her favorite dress would have to be altered before she could wear it again in public.

Sighing, Jenna pulled out her sewing box. She rummaged around until her fingers found the correct shade of thread. A golden yellow that would match the dress perfectly.

She unwound the thread, snipping it efficiently. Turning towards the light she held the needle up and started to thread the gold through the eye…

And froze.

Clickety Clackety. Click. Clack. Click. Clack.

She could hear the spinning wheel as if she were there in the dungeon, desperately crafting simple straw into gold once more. Sweat dripping off her brow, knowing what price she would pay for failure.

Miserly Wiserly. Miserly Wiserly. Miser. Wiser.

One who was a miser, who used to be wise. Someone her trust had been given to, just as surely as he had broken it. He should have protected them, and instead had betrayed them for spun gold.

Shaking, Jenna dropped thread and needle. A moan wrenched itself from her throat as she felt the world shift beneath her and she collapsed onto the floor.

The name's the game. The name's your game. Name game.

A choice, not of her own making. A kind voice saying "Freedom has its price. Are you willing to pay it?"

Her own voice crying out against it. But it was not her bargain to be made.

The blue eyes that she would recognize anywhere, boring deep into hers. "She will remember…"

Spinning out of time.

She rose to her knees, tears cascading down her face. He had been right after all. She did remember. She remembered their cottage, the silver and gold ring that he had placed on her finger. She remembered the gentle wizard cautioning him against such a course, telling him that world walking was difficult both in the coming and the going, with no guarantee that she could be *found,* let alone return. Jenna remembered the pain etched on his face when she had been stolen from him.

But the bitch of it, the absolute worst of it, was that she still did not remember his name. She knew his body intimately, knew every scar he carried and how he had received them. She knew that if she stole a sip of Irish Crème coffee he would caress her hand just *so* as he reclaimed his cup. And that caress would precede a kiss in which they shared the rich taste of the coffee. Truth be told, she would steal a sip of the steaming liquid just for the kiss.

But the name was the game. The game that she *had* to win. There would be no prize for remembering his caress, for remembering their life together. It was the name or nothing.

Jenna crawled to her room and pulled herself up onto her bed. Curling onto her side, she clutched a pillow tightly to her breast and soaked it with her tears.

***

Jenna's life did not resume its normal pace. After work, she roamed the streets, looking into beggars' eyes trying to find a set that could see into her soul. She found herself wandering into coffee shops at odd times, ordering Irish Crème.

Bookshops became a favorite haunt, as well. She would pick up books of baby names, carry them clutched tightly against her chest until she got back to her apartment.

Once she arrived at home, she would open the book and scour through the names. None of them rang true.

It was one such night when he returned to her. She was curled up on the sofa, the lamp light just enough to spill over onto the pages of the book. She fingered the cup of coffee on the side table absently.

And felt his caress.

He was not alone this time. An older man, resembling in looks if not attire the beggar he had pretended to be, stood beside him. Jenna grinned wryly. "Good evening, Wizard Thornlock."

"And to you, Mistress Jenna." The wizard's voice rumbled through his throat. His eyes gentled as they looked on her. "You know why we are here, then?"

Jenna nodded her head slowly. She wanted to beg for more time, a clue, anything to make this easier. "Won't you have a seat?"

The wizard perched on the edge of her coffee table. *He* sat on the couch next to her. She leaned into his warmth as he reached around her and picked up the cup of coffee.

"Do you remember, then?" His voice was soft against her ear.

"I remember so much. I remember the bargain you struck against my will." Her voice surprised her in its steadiness.

"I had to, lass. I couldna let him abuse you so."

She nodded her head. "But remembering our life isn't enough, is it? I have to know your name as well."

She felt a shudder run through him. She looked directly into Thornlock's eyes, unwavering. "Am I permitted to ask a question?"

Thornlock nodded slowly. "As long as you do not attempt to ask his name."

She thought carefully over the memories that had blossomed in her. She could remember him, remember incidents. But she couldn't remember... "By what name do you call me?"

"Ach, now, lassie, you know I call you wife."

Jenna breathed deeply, evenly. Her answer could leave them worse off than before. If she failed...

"Then I have no choice but to call you... husband."

Thornlock's laughter was immediate and chilling. Sobbing, Jenna covered her eyes with her hands. She would lose him. Had lost him. He would never caress her hand gently, she would never feel his hungry lips on hers again.

Jenna sat, listening to the beating of her own heart for several minutes. 'Twould have been much easier if she had been allowed to forget than to endure the heartache. Much easier to forget than to remember marriage to Llewellyn.

Llewellyn.

Her eyes snapped open and were blinded by sudden the onslaught of sunlight. "Llewellyn!"

Slowly, things came back into focus. Instead of the sofa in her apartment, she was sitting in a deep chair in front of a fireplace. Ceiling beams arched above her head. Taking a deep breath, she could smell the trees from the grove just outside the door. Fresh, tangy, crisp air filled her lungs.

"Llewellyn?"

"Ach, now, lass, can't a body get himself a cup o' coffee?" His voice was tender, gentle.

Jenna stood and walked across the room to him. Holding his gaze, she took the cup from him and took a small sip.

Irish Crème.

With a smile, he took the cup back, caressing her hand just so.

Dog Days
(Carl Hughes)

As ulcers go, this has been a humdinger. It's eaten through the lining of Mia's stomach and gnawed into a blood vessel. Not good. The result has been massive internal bleeding, dizziness that makes vertigo seem like a walk in the park, convulsive vomiting of revolting and stinking black stuff, and a rush to hospital in an ambulance. Now, cannula in her wrist and blood type O dripping into her veins, Mia is feeling a bit more perky. The oxygen they've stuffed up her nostrils has helped and the blood is slowly restoring a flush to her parchment cheeks.

'What's the matter with you, my love?' asks an old dear in the next bed. The glossy board above the bed declares her to be called Assunta Creak, a patient of Dr Roxanne Tremlett.

'I've a vicious ulcer that's decided to eat my stomach,' Mia says.

'An ulcer? Bit young for that, aren't you? What are you – twenty? Twenty-one?'

'Twenty-five actually. I blame my job. It's stressful.'

'I'm three score years and plenty and have never had an ulcer, touch wood.' She taps her head. 'But my Graham suffered from ulcers all his life, poor pet. One burst eventually and killed him.'

'Thanks a lot,' Mia says.

'Oh, I didn't mean to suggest that's what'll happen to you. Like as not they'll pump something into you and you'll be skipping around in no time.'

There are six beds in this alcove, five of them occupied by aged women like Assunta Creak. One of them is snoring, sounding like a rhinoceros giving birth. Another resembles a corpse that's seen better days.

A nurse with rosebud lips arrives to check the plastic bag containing Mia's blood and she says brightly, 'We'll soon have you as good as new. Dr Parkinson'll be along shortly to talk to you about treatment and so on.'

'It's the so on that bothers me,' Mia says.

The nurse giggles. Her name tag says *Hermione*. 'There's a lot of so-ons in here, but don't worry. You've nothing to be scared of. We'll get rid of that nasty ulcer for good and all.'

Dr Parkinson arrives ten minutes later. He's a greying man with a smile like treacle and a nose like a lupin. As he leans over Mia she gets a whiff of body odour that resembles regurgitated cabbage.

'You'll need five units of blood because you've bled massively inside,' he says merrily, as if discussing the installation of a Christmas tree. 'Then we'll give you medication that'll allow the ulcer to heal quickly. You're a victim of h.pylori, which sounds scarier than it is. It just means you have a bug that needs to be blasted away with antibiotics. Once those beasts have gone you'll forget you ever suffered from an ulcer.'

'The young lady has a stressful job, doc – that's what's brought this on,' Assunta Creak chimes in.

'What are you – a brain surgeon?' the doctor asks Mia with a smile.

'Nothing as noble as that. I'm a legal executive.'

'A legal eagle, eh? You'll soon be legally eagling again, trust me. My job isn't as stressful as yours. I pretend to work and they pretend to pay me.' He titters into a horny hand. 'Anyway, for now, we'll change this bag of claret that's dripping into your veins and settle you down for the night. You'll feel much better by morning.'

It's well known that hospitals at night are among the noisiest places on Earth, so it's said that if you need a good night's rest when you're ill, don't go into hospital. Nurses usually spend the night shouting to each other, clattering about, wheeling squeaky trolleys, banging drawers. But Mia has a wonderful night's sleep, which is as pleasing as it is surprising.

The ward lights come on at six-thirty next morning and Mia emerges blearily from a dream about nothing worth recalling. After a minute, yawning, she sits up and sees that her bag of blood has been renewed. She stretches and looks around the alcove. Then she freezes, breath petrified in her throat. For the other patients have all developed dogs' heads during the night.

Assunta Creak looks precisely the same as she did yesterday except for her head, which is now that of a Shetland sheepdog. Across the ward, the woman who'd been snoring has become a beagle with long floppy ears, while the patient who'd resembled a corpse is a chihuahua. The other two women are respectively a Dalmatian and a Yorkshire terrier.

'What is this?' Mia demands. 'Are we putting on a fancy-dress show?'

The women, or dogs or whatever, stare at her.

'You're a peculiar-looking thing,' Assunta says.

'Gross!' declares the Yorkshire terrier.

Frantic, Mia delves into a bag at the side of her bed, rummages around and produces her hand mirror. Dreading what she'll see, she holds it in front of her face. But she looks as she always has. Human to the core. Not pretty, not plain. Just Mia.

'Nurse?' She calls the word tremulously. This is probably a joke but instead of amusing her it's got her as jittery as windy shadows under a waning moon.

A couple of nurses enter the ward. One has the head of a chow chow and the other a dobermann.

'What's the problem?' the dobermann asks, coming to Mia's bedside.

'Why's everybody wearing dog masks?' Mia asks.

'Masks?' The nurse emits a slobbering giggle. 'You are a caution. Don't fret, Mia – you'll be looking just like everyone else soon.'

'Am I suffering from a brain tumour?' Mia asks, halfway to panic. 'Am I hallucinating? Everyone I'm looking at has a dog's head.'

'Well, of course they have,' the nurse says as if talking to a toddler who's afraid of things lurking in wardrobes. 'That's why you're in hospital, isn't it? To remedy your deficiency.'

'I'm in hospital because of a stomach ulcer,' Mia protests.

'That too, of course. Anyway, here's Dr Parkinson. He wants to see you before he goes off duty.'

The doctor approaches. Mia shrinks from him because he has the head of a shih tzu. He's all hair and droopy whiskers.

'Now then, Mia, I can see you're alarmed about undergoing surgery but there's really no need to worry,' he says. The words dribble out of his dog's mouth like wet syllables. 'Wonderful advances have been made in medical science so it's now possible for you to have a head transplant. Have you any preference for the type of dog you'd like to be?'

Mia feels as if her insides are being mangled and crushed beneath a steamroller. She recoils, frantic. 'I must be going mad!' she blurts. 'I don't want to look like a dog!'

'Of course you do,' the doctor says sternly. 'You've no wish to go on being the odd one out, have you? You don't want everyone to stare! Now look, I've brought a brochure with lots of pictures of dogs' heads. You can choose whichever one you like. We do a very nice line in Pekes or golden retrievers. Or perhaps you're more of a borzoi or boxer. I don't recommend the basset hound – too dopey looking. Mind you, border collies are becoming very popular, with or without erect ears. Anyway, the choice is yours. Don't let me influence you.'

'Disconnect me from this bag of blood,' Mia says with an intensity that could smash rocks. 'I've had enough of this charade. I'm leaving.'

'Oh, we can't disconnect you, my dear,' the dobermann nurse says. She exchanges a patronising smile with the doctor. 'It could lead to an embolism and that'd kill you for sure.'

'Ah, here's Dr Gloria Mattock and her surgical colleagues,' Dr Parkinson says as a rottweiler approaches with a team of Staffordshire bull terriers.

Dr Mattock has lambent eyes and drooling chops. Mia once saw eyes like those in a newspaper cartoon and they reminded her of spirits walking in haunted hallways. Nothing has changed.

'Mia can't decide what head to adopt,' Dr Parkinson informs the surgeon.

'Never mind,' Dr Mattock says. 'We'll select an appropriate one for you, my dear. It'll be a nice surprise when you wake up from the operation.'

'I don't want to look like a dog!' Mia screams the words and propels herself as far into the bed as she can, as if it will swallow her and remove her to Wonderland.

'Just listen to the racket that stupid woman's making,' complains the chihuahua.

'She's a tasteless specimen I must say,' declares Assunta the Sheltie.

The Staffordshire bull terriers move in, grasp Mia's arms so she can't move, and Dr Mattock injects something from a hypodermic syringe the size of the Royal Albert Hall.

Blackness envelops her. Time passes in a vacuum. Then there's the sound of rushing, like a waterfall over crystal, and her vision comes swimmingly into view.

She's back on the ward, no longer connected to the blood bag. A nurse with the face of a pug is standing over her with a mirror.

'Welcome back, Mia,' she says brightly. 'Now you can look at yourself and see what a remarkable job Dr Mattock's done.'

She holds up a square mirror and Mia screws her eyes shut. But only for a moment. Then she opens them and sees looking back at her the face of an Irish wolfhound. She screams, blabbering, grasps the air as if it's something to prevent her drowning.

'From now on you'll pass unnoticed,' the nurse says. 'There's nothing worse than being the only one of your type. And of course this is only a day procedure – no need to keep you incarcerated here. You can go home now.'

Mia hardly registers what happens during the next half hour. Her brain seems to have developed as much substance as a congealed omelette. Somehow she dresses herself, stumbles out of the ward, through the corridors, seeing dogs all the way.

Then she's out on the street where a frigid wind is blowing and it seems to pass right through her. And children scream, and adults stare and grimace and recoil.

'You poor, poor deformed thing,' says one woman with rouge on her cheeks and a smear of scarlet lipstick. 'You look just like a dog. Can't they do anything for you in the hospital?'

Lucifer and the Large Hadron Collider
(Ian McKinley)

The boffins in the Geneva control room claimed that they expected the unexpected when the Large Hadron Collider energy ramped up after its latest upgrade. In all honesty, though, that did not include the small silver sphere that materialised just above the master control panel with a barely audible pop. As almost everyone present was following the action there, a babble of shocked exclamations, screams and curses almost drowned out the mellifluous baritone that issued from it. "You rang?"

While the cautious were running towards exits and the sceptical were searching for hints on how this prank had been pulled off, one young physicist merely stared at the levitating ball with a frown of serious concentration. "ET, I'll bet," she finally muttered under her breath.

More cries of consternation resulted as the object of her interest moved slowly in her direction, parting a sea of academics like a high-tech Moses.

"OK, you'll do! You seem a bit smarter than the average bear in these parts. How would you like the job of spokesman for planet Earth?"

The brow of the red-haired girl wrinkled again as she considered the question that was evidently being posed to her, apparently unperturbed by the incongruity of the situation or the growing disruption caused by a couple of bigwigs in expensive suits who were fighting to get closer to the action.

"From your mastery of idiom, you clearly know what you're letting yourself in for," she answered in a deliberate tone. "OK, spokeswoman would be fine for me."

"Spokeswoman it is!" The voice radiated warmth, as if struggling to contain a chuckle. "What a good start, politically incorrect within a minute of arrival!"

The volume of the voice didn't increase at all, but instead of being localised at the sphere it now appeared to issue throughout the huge room. "Maureen McNeil is now my official liaison with your world. It might be good for some of you older guys to sort out the international diplomatic bunfight that'll result from this first contact. In addition, some of your techies should get started putting together the evidence that'll be needed. Measuring my mass should do it: how about if I set it as a nice round million kilogrammes? In the interim, Maureen and I'll have a chat."

A faint shimmer defined a volume enclosing the sphere and the young woman, cutting out external sound completely and leaving the odd pair in total silence.

"You're grinning," the alien observed.

"It was just your mention of my name threw me, but then I realised that you must be able to hack any database that we possess, so it can't be too hard to identify me."

"Yes, the colour of your hair would make that an easy job, even if you weren't wearing a name badge."

Maureen's grin widened.

"So, have you any questions before we start?"

"I had been wondering if you were alive or some form of AI, but I guess that might not be politically correct on my part."

Once again, the visitor sounded amused. "I'm not sure that I could answer that anyway, your language just doesn't contain the appropriate concepts."

"And would you respond the same way if I asked where you came from?"

"Wow, you really are much smarter than your compatriots!"

Maureen looked pleased by the complement, but was still clearly struggling to nail down some concern. Her question, however, seemed an afterthought. "What do I call you; do you have a name?"

"Very perceptive question! A name would be good thing to have hereabouts. What about Lucifer?"

The young woman laughed delightedly. "OK, Lightbringer, let's get started."

"Compared to the chaos outside, you seem very calm," Lucifer observed. Indeed, there seemed to be a lot going on, as the glowing aura around them was clearly some kind of force field that was resisting all efforts to approach within its boundary.

"I read lots of comics. This is buttons compared to some of the weird shit I'm regularly exposed to."

"Although being dosed up to the eyeballs with this Valium stuff probably helps."

42

"Shit, the presentation this afternoon! I don't suppose that matters much now, though."

"I doubt it. Anyway, so what do you think is going to happen now?"

"Well, you've appointed me spokeswoman, so I guess you want to speak to me about something."

The silence stretched, so the redhead continued. "You can probably access everything about mankind that's available electronically, which must be just about everything there is to know. In that case, I would think you must want personal input from an individual, maybe as a basis for some decision that you've got to make."

"You hit the nail directly on the head. You're on a roll here: so what's the decision?"

"Is this a chat or a test?" The retort was softened by a smile. "Anyway, I love tests, even if I'm not very good at speaking in public. So, let's see..."

She counted the points on the fingers of her right hand while she scowled in concentration.

"The timing of your arrival and your cryptic comment indicate that the LHC set whatever is now happening in motion. We rang: that must be some kind of signal that's produced when a certain energy threshold is passed, tachyons or something."

"Or something," Lucifer agreed.

"And this must be an indicator of technology reaching a critical level: we have become worthy of notice by more advanced civilisations." A second finger was stroking her lower lip.

"Worthy?"

"Mmm, yes, that's a point. Depends what you would represent in human terms. Maybe you could be an envoy offering us membership in an intergalactic council."

Lucifer let out an amazingly human snort, conveying more than speech could possibly do.

"I didn't really think that was likely to be the case, but it was a possibility. Another could be that you are a wandering anthropologist who has come to study the monkeys who have just managed to chip flint. That wouldn't require much of a decision beyond determining whether we are worth wasting any more of your time on."

No response, so Maureen continued. "More worryingly, you could be here because the monkeys have just discovered fire and you're going to nail them down before they burn down the bloody forest."

"All good guesses, but not quite on the mark. You have reached a critical level of technology, but you clearly don't know how to apply it."

"As indicated by the way that we're currently screwing up our planet!"

"Yes, that'd be a good example. An amazing number of primitive societies do manage to make themselves extinct before becoming civilised. Indeed, in more densely populated parts, they often make a lot of other species extinct in the process."

"You mean that it is possible to reach interplanetary travel level, without being civilised?"

The snort was even louder this time. "Interspecies, interplanetary or interstellar genocide can be managed with the most basic technology –

and technology, per se, has nothing to do with civilisation in any case. Complete barbarians have mastered intergalactic teleportation: it's just a matter of sums and a bit of engineering," Lucifer concluded dismissively.

Maureen now looked a little disturbed. "But we rang a bell, just with that," a thumb pointed in the direction of the LHC control board, as if she was wanting to hitch a lift in that direction. "I guess your kids play with toys like that in kindergarten."

"We don't do kids, but you're certainly right, it's a real Heath Robinson approach to examining sub-atomic structure. But the aim is the main thing…" There was an expectant pause that made it clear that the quiz was continuing.

"Mmm, investing huge resources to bugger about doing something fundamentally useless?" she ventured.

"Yes, well that's certainly a concise way of putting it." Lucifer sounded amused by this answer. "It's an indication of a certain maturity of Weltanschauung and thus it could mean that your species has some potential."

"Notwithstanding that we appear barbaric in almost every other way," the redhead interrupted.

"Are actually barbaric in every other way!" The bite of the statement was reduced by the hint of a laugh. "Let's just call it sneaking over the line in the sand defining the emergence of sentience."

"Well, at least it's nice to know that this bloody monstrosity has actually produced something worthwhile as a spinoff. After a couple of years in this nut-house I was beginning to wonder if I had made the right career choice."

"Do you think you would have progressed further with your summer pole-dancing and the OnlyFans stuff?"

"Rhetorical question! If academics were paid properly, I wouldn't need to moonlight." Maureen broke in, turning slightly pink. She may be within a sound-cancelling force field, but there were some topics better not discussed with multiple levels of CERN's upper hierarchy crammed around. "Anyway, it seems that you're checking up on some atom-smashing monkeys. You can't be looking for information from me, as I'm sure that anything that you could want is already available to you."

"No?" The question hung in the air, just like the sphere did.

"Bugger! I forgot that I was the appointed spokeswoman. This means that you're looking for a statement from me, which could be my opinion or a decision on behalf of Mankind?"

"The latter probably comes closest to what I need."

"Shit! I knew you were going to say that. Don't you think that I might be a little under-qualified for a decision that must be truly monumental in scope? Wouldn't you rather have a top politician or something."

A distinctly nasal snort was followed by clarification. "Remember that the fact of some members of your troop of monkeys reaching a level that might just be mistaken for sentient shouldn't be

46

taken as a generalisation that extends to the mental runts of the pack."

"Point made, but I'm still not qualified."

"Undoubtedly!"

The physicist waited for more, but Lucifer was clearly much more adept in this game than she was. "OK, I need to do something that I'm completely incapable of..." Still no response from the sphere. She scowled and continued, "Or, maybe, something that I'm not yet capable of?"

"Excellent, I knew you'd get there. We just need to look at some places and give you a bit more background and then you'll be ready to rock and roll." There seemed to be a definite tone of smug satisfaction in this announcement.

"And how much time would that take?"

"Taking time, what a truly bizarre idea." The accompanying laugh indicated pleasure in the concept rather than being in any way scathing. "I do see what you mean, though. How much time would you like it to take?"

Maureen answered slowly, speaking her thoughts as she worked her way through this riddle. "Well, it's true that time is a bit of a woolly concept, especially as you evidently have faster-than-light transport or something similar."

"I'm not sure that it's similar to anything that you'd call FTL transport, but it certainly isn't slower than light," Lucifer interrupted.

The redhead nodded as if this simply confirmed her speculation. "In that case, there could be quite a difference between the elapsed time on the planet Earth timeline and what I would perceive during our

47

little jolly. Let me put it this way: how long would I think our trip would take if I was counting it in earth years?"

"Maybe a millennium or two, give or take."

"Shit!" The inadvertent ejaculation seemed shrill even to Maureen's ears. She tried to calm herself before she continued. "Now you know I'm talking about real, perceived time and not something complicated by relativistic time compression?"

"Of course; although I don't know what you think is so real about it."

"Let's not get into that at present. You must understand that I'm not built with that kind of longevity!"

"Oh, the meat bit," Lucifer laughed again. "No, we don't need that – I only need you. If we need physical presence anywhere, then we have this sphere."

"Wouldn't it be a bit cramped? Bugger! No don't even bother to tell me that 3D space is another of our quaint monkey concepts."

The chuckle was confirmation enough, so she continued. "Right, let's see if I can get my head round this. I need to shuffle off my mortal coil and jaunt off with you for a millennium."

"Give or take."

"Ah, yes, I'd forgotten about that suspicious caveat. Give or take what? A couple of centuries, a millennium, more?"

"These kinds of processes are tricky to nail down in your language…"

If a floating sphere could be said to be shuffling its feet, that was what it was doing, Maureen decided. "OK, nail it down as best you can."

"Well, let's say give or take an order of magnitude; or two, just to be on the safe side."

"So, we could be off on our travels for up to a hundred thousand years!" Now her voice was distinctly hysterical.

"Maybe something like that. After all there's a lot to learn and quite a few places to see."

"A hundred thousand years! After that time there'd be nothing left on earth that I would remotely recognise," she mused out loud, still in a state of shock. Then she realised that she had almost missed a snort from Lucifer's direction. "Wait a minute, what would the elapsed time be on earth's timeline."

"What would you like it to be? Pick any positive number."

"Pick any positive… Hold on, you're implying that we're going to step outside our timeline and can return at any time. Also, you seem to imply that travel backwards in time is impossible."

"Time, time, time! Why do you biologicals get so worked up about this parameter? OK, let's just say that we can step back here a bit later, whenever you choose, and that moving to an earlier part of the timeline is a bit trickier in this universe."

"In this universe? How many are there?"

"How many do you want there to be?"

"Damn it! For an omnipotent ET, you can be a right pain in the arse at times."

"Yes, but omnipotent only in this universe at this particular time!" The associated girlish giggle seemed designed to be particularly annoying.

"Right, well I'm not going to go there either! You and I will jaunt off for the eons that I will need to make a decision on behalf of my planet, then come back and let everyone know what I've decided. I guess there'll be a lot of pissed-off bigwigs when I break that news."

"What you do when you get back, if and when you do, is completely up to you. You just have to make your choice and then that's it as far as I'm concerned."

"This is quite tricky for me to take in. For someone more used to three score and ten as a personal lifetime duration, heading off for millennia is a bit of a jump in the dark. Then again, it must be pretty important if you're prepared to dedicate that amount of time to me."

"There we go again with time," the sphere issued a weary sigh. "And, also, dedication of it. I can assure you that the limited response capacity that you see here is due to multi-tasking. You're only one of the low-level species that I'm looking after."

"Oh, how many are there?" asked the young physicist, diverted from her original topic of conversation by this titbit of unexpected knowledge.

"In this universe, no more than a few thousand," Lucifer sounded apologetic, adding, "after all it has a short timeline and its mathematical basis, physics you call it, is rather restrictive."

"And how many universes are there?"

"How many do you want…?"

"OK, OK, I've got you on counting universes," Maureen interrupted, rubbing her face while she tried to marshal her thoughts. "Anyway, regardless of numbers, this has got to be a very important decision that I have to make."

"I'm sure some of your fellow monkeys would think so."

"Only some? I thought this was a really big deal – something like life or death of planet Earth."

"Well, technically, it's quite a lot bigger than that."

"What? The solar system, our local star cluster, the Milky Way?"

"Getting a bit warmer."

The following chuckle was infuriating, but Maureen was still trying to recover from the shock of this revelation of impending doom. "A galactic scale catastrophe, how is that even possible?"

"Well, when I said getting warmer, I was referring only to the impact on this particular universe."

"Jesus! Multi-universe scale catastrophe! Where the hell could that come from?" She scratched her head in frustration as the silence drew out. "That's something like intersection of 4D branes," she eventually suggested.

"Good girl! I knew you'd get there if I gave you a couple of hints. The 4D bit is rather simplistic, but it's certainly going in the right general direction."

"I'd do a lot of swearing now if my brain wasn't boiling so much that I can't find the appropriate vocabulary. It's just too much to take in."

"That's why we need to pop out and look at a few things and get you up to speed. After that, there's no problem."

"So, we'll be able to stop the brane intersection?"

"What?" The question seemed to have surprised Lucifer so much that the sphere appeared to quiver. "No, no, no! Doing anything to influence branes is so far above my sentience level that I don't even know if it is fundamentally possible or not. The very best we can do is minimise the consequences for your species to a small extent."

"Wait a minute, you said before that this would worry only a few of my fellow monkeys."

"I'm sure there would be some, but not a lot. It's quite general with newly emerging races, especially the biological ones. It seems to come with short personal timelines and institutionalised mythologies."

"I think I'm slowly getting the hang of Lucifer-speak," Maureen mused. "So, when you've explained the situation to other biological sentients, how many of them go walkabout with you?"

"Not a lot, a few percent."

It seemed like a reluctant confession to young Doctor McNeil's ears. "Any you think this is to do with short lives and religions. Let's start with timelines; on Earth's when will this catastrophe take place?"

"Relatively soon."

This time it was Maureen doing the waiting. "Okay, about a million of your years, give or take."

"That'd be plus or minus about two orders of magnitude, I'd guess," she responded, smugly.

"About that."

"I can understand why most races would be rather unconcerned then."

"The organic ones: most others can see this in a proper context."

"I don't think I'm ready for inorganic species quite yet," the redhead smiled, feeling for the first time that she was really getting the hang of communicating with the ET. "Let's get back to the mythologies; God-bothering as I like to refer to it. This is also a factor constraining uptake on your offer. Why would that be?"

"You're the monkey, what do you think?" Lucifer was clearly trying to regain the initiative.

"Well, the great unwashed may prefer to pray to God rather than trust a dodgy space robot, if they even thought its Cassandra tale was plausible in the first place."

"This is certainly a factor, although most intelligent species would spot that I am a bit more than a space robot!"

"Just teasing," Maureen chuckled, enjoying the opportunity for flippancy with an almost omnipotent entity. "Okay, the other thing might be actually going off with the diabolical ET. Just how does that work exactly?"

The silence dragged out. Maureen realised that this meant that there had been enough hints for her to work it out for herself. She tried to replay their conversation in her mind in as much detail as she could. Luckily her memory was very good and a somewhat scary picture began to build up.

"The name you selected was a clue, wasn't it?" No response, so she continued, "You want me to go off with you, but you don't seem to want my physical body; I seem to remember you called it the meaty part or something similar. So, you want my soul?"

"It is quite a nice concept, isn't it. Most meat intelligences go through a phase of mystifying their essence. I suppose because they don't hang onto it very long. I could certainly describe it better, but you don't have the maths, or at least you don't have it yet."

"A mathematical quantification of the soul, that would really screw with the minds of a lot of God-botherers I know. Anyway, you're coming along with a Faustian deal: my immortal soul for inconceivable knowledge?"

"Well, the analogy was the closest I could find in the mythology that you're familiar with, but you can take it a bit too far. Your soul isn't anything like immortal and I don't want to have it, just borrow it for a little."

"You use a little in a context that is truly alien, you know, but how can I be sure this isn't a double bluff and that you aren't actually a demon from the pit?"

"You really believe that mumbo-jumbo?"

"Of course not! Just joking. But anyway, now that the role playing's over, what's your real name."

"Well, your concept of names doesn't match mine and you don't have the maths in any case. If I tried to translate into your number system, it would start with aleph-six and then get complicated."

"Aleph, that's a good start. I'd prefer to sell my soul to somebody called that."

"Not sell, if anything, rent," Aleph interjected.

"OK, rent. In any case, I don't think I could pass on this chance, even if I ended up saving Earth only as a by-product."

"You won't actually save Earth…"

"OK, save my species…" Maureen ignored the groan and continued, "…or whatever I'm supposed to do. Anyway, I'm sure that it'll all be a lot clearer when I have the math in a century or two. Right then: beam me up, Scotty!"

Maureen somehow recognised that the full transition from stereoscopic visual to four pi multispectral was being sheltered from her, but she was shocked to see her body in the process of collapsing to the floor. "Shit, that's me, I'm dead!"

"Oh, the meat, do you really want to keep that?"

"Bloody right I do. That's my body!"

"No problem, I'll just put it in stasis and shove a force field around it. You probably won't want it though."

"Well, if I do, at least it'll be here."

"When do you want to come back to this timeline?"

"Not too long and not too short. How about 3 days and 3 nights?"

A long-suffering sigh was accompanied by sotto voce, "Monkeys and their mythologies!"

"OK, Faust, make it so!"

There was a barely audible pop, leaving chaos in the LHC control room surrounding the impenetrably-screened corpse.

Ninja Kitty
(Jackk N. Killington)

I am like the wind. Gentle strides as I race, dark and deadly upon the wall that separates the Shinden-Zukuri from the rest of the village, and the world beyond. The townspeople in their squalid homes that the Daimyo claimed to care for, working and slaving for the Samurai and their corrupted, cruel lord lived just outside, fending for themselves in a world both cruel and unforgiving.

His samurai, a collection of Sakhalin, Akita, and Kai-ken walked the yard below. Guarding the inner and outer gates were a pair of Tigrettes, comprising only some of Lord Kuro's most trusted troops. Their large striped frames fierce in the torchlight as they stood and watched for intrusions.

The region had not fared well under Daimyo Kuro's rule, and bands of Fe' and Ca' had rose up against the tyrannical lord, but they had not been enough, and I had passed them slung from ropes in the trees, or chained to their bases, brutalized in the fashion of our previous masters. The indignity added to the injustice that Kuro liked to pass off as rule of law. I had passed too many dead on my way to this nobleman's fortification. Too many.

I look at the night sky. The moon is dark this night, hidden with the rest of the stars above by heavy clouds that threatened a night of terrors. A perfect night for an assassination, I think as I slip down from the wall, evading the lights of the torches with ease, and start making my way down the inner wall towards the second guard house.

I walk swiftly but cautiously, all the while keeping a look out for the Itatsi that burrow and wait for someone unknown to cross their path. The shogun's pets and an added security force. There were only two that I saw, playing with the Akita guards on the west end of the home, while I watched a Kai-ken turn the corner of the other side of the home, disappearing from sight. I had watched them all for a moment from within a bush, and now I step out, moving to the pond and following its edge to the pavilion, staying as far from the torchlight and the Samurai as I could. Capture was certain death, and I had no intent upon dying this night.

I jumped on the railing of the pavilion and heard the scuffling of an approaching Itatsi in the walkway. I crouched on the railing on the side of the little building as the weasel raised its head and cocked it to the wind, trying to make out the many smells that the night allotted him, but as I pulled a poisoned dart from my belt, I could tell that it had sensed me, but could not smell me. The wind was in my favor. I thanked my ancestors as the weasel turned and scuttled off towards the main house. Once I felt safe, I raised myself to the roof and made my way towards the Shinden Hall, hunched low enough that the guards did not see me from their vantage points.

My hearing was exceptional, even for a Fe' of my lineage, and I could hear voices passing through the wood roof and paper walls. The Sparrow floors creaked as someone inside paced. "The Neko have started to revolt in the south Daimyo Kuro." The voice had a slither to it. I knew that it was his Prime Advisor Kai. His advisories as venomous as his Komodo bite.

"Those ferals?" I heard Kuro's voice. "My dear, dear Kai," Kuro laughed. "My forces could eradicate the lot of them in, I would say, barely an afternoon. The rabble will always rabble, and sometimes the rabble too much, and get razed."

"But sir, I beg you to heed caution."

"Folly, my guards keep me safe, and they will always be as faithful as the gold I pay them, and I do pay them well." Kuro laughed again. "You worry too much advisor, we are safe within these walls."

"Well, Daimyo, that is my job." Kai said.

I unslung my bow and took out my rope and grappling hook, tying the rope around my waist and then attached the hook to the tip of the roof. I looked to see that I hadn't been spotted, and then started to lower myself down head first. Two arrows drawn from my quiver, with one notched upon the string.

The Tigrette had been motionless, soundless as he'd stood guard before the open door to the hall, and the lords inside. I do not know why I had not expected this, but regardless, he was not expecting me. Upon seeing the Tigrette, I let myself fall quickly. I unnotched the arrow and plunged it into the guard's eye so quickly that he had had no time to raise even the utterance of alarm.

Kuro and Kai had drawn silent as their guard dropped, shocked at what was happening, but before the body had hit the floor, my arrow was renotched to the string and the first of the two had been let loose. The first of the arrows, bloodied by his guard, hit Daimyo Kuro in the throat. His eyes widened as he fell back from his kneeling mat. Gagging and dying even as he hit the ground.

Kai stood opened mouth as he looked at his lord fall, and then, with a stupefied look, maw wide, he looked up to see me notching back the second arrow and letting it fly. The arrow found purchase through Kai's opened mouth and out the back of his neck. He also fell backwards to lay next to his already dead lords body as he gagged and tried pulling the arrow out of his throat.

I pulled myself back up and walked to where I had hooked my grapple to the point in the roof. As I dislodged it from the bamboo I felt a whisper in my ear and heard a thunk as one of the guards arrows hit and dug into the bamboo roof. All around me the world exploded. They had found the dead guards on the other side of the wall. They had found me.

There were five samurai on the wall now, they were notching their arrows and letting them loose at me, while others were raising the alarms. More arrows thudded into the wood around me as two Itatsi's climbed onto the roof and started loping towards me, their mouths frothing as the prospects of my death and possible ingestion flooded their minds. I would not give them the chance, I thought as I danced on the roof, not giving the samurai a still target to fire upon. I reached down to my thigh and pulled out two Kunai from the holder that I had there; I let them fly with all the deadly precision that my training allotted me. The Itatsi dropped as my blades sank into them. I started running then.

Leaping onto the canopied walkway of the pavilion and racing down its length back towards the pond. Two Akita's had made their way upon the pavilion and were drawing their weapons as I raced towards them. I put forth a burst of speed that they were not expecting. Pulling my wakizashi and slicing them both as I passed them and jumped onto the grounds below.

I was at the wall within seconds, using my claws to pull myself up to the perimeter walkway. As I stood on the wood, looking at guards that barked and growled and roared as they gave chase, I pulled a shuriken from my pocket and threw it at the first of the guards. It hit the dog in the chest and he dropped, the Akita behind him tripped over his comrade as I leapt from the wall, running the short distance between the Shinden and the wooded lands beyond. I was too fast for their arrows to find me, and by the time I reached the woods, my only thought was the eagerness to be home, and to tell my Sifu the story of a job well done. A night of sleep, and tomorrow, back to training.

I am the night. I am the darkness. I am death.

I am Sprinkles, the ninja kitty.

Flotsam
(Liam A Spinage)

People talk about the calm before the storm like a time of profound peace that is about to be shattered irrevocably. They nod as they do so, their eyes promising wisdom as their mouth delivers nothing but drivel. You'll notice, of course, that this only works in hindsight. You don't know it's the calm before the storm at the time because you don't know that the storm is coming. Or, if you do, you don't know when or how long it will last, how much damage it will cause.

People only talk about the calm before the storm once the storm has passed and they're picking up wreckage of their broken ships, homes, and lives. That calm is imaginary; it's pure nostalgia, you could bottle it as such and sell it at one of the local night markets.

There's no calm before a storm. You thought the last few days were calm, when the town was sweltering? When everyone was cooking their evening meal with their windows wide open, pans sizzling and tantalising passers-by as the aroma wafted into the street? When everyone forgot just for a while that their hatches weren't battened down and played music and sang and argued and cursed as if their place was shut up tight against the coming winter and all their thoughts were private?

Every one of those people was brimming with frenzied anticipation, whether they were longing for rainy relief or making hay while the sun still shone. Look beneath the surface and you'll see no calm, no mere ripples; instead a sultry seething, a boiling of blood. They don't call them heated arguments for no reason.

After the storm, that's when it's calm. Once the clouds have broken and the rain has evaporated and the people are cool again, their simmering sensibilities having bubbled over and then spilled out onto the docks only to be washed away in the morning tide. Windows stay closed, music goes unheard in the streets outside and all you can hear is the endless battle for dominance between the wood pigeons and the gulls.

As the clouds part and the skies shudders back to normalcy, so do the denizens of the little coastal town of Esperanza.

At least, that's what usually happens. The storms are regular enough that people set the seasons by them, sing songs, and tell tales about them, turn them into heroes and villains, even rely on them for their livelihood. They fear and worship those awesome, awful storms in equal measure. On occasion, though, something different happens. The patterns break, the waves break, the routine breaks. In these times, there is no calm before, during or after the storm. You can't be calm when you're in peril.

**

"Mama, Papa, come see!"

Their daughters often played on the beach in the evening when the sun was cooler and brought back little treasures: shells, seaweed, odd-looking bits of flotsam that washed up on the shore which had twisted into interesting shapes, the gossipings of fisherfolk and the stories they carried with them of brave and happy corsairs, fierce pirates, huge beasts of the bay which lived beneath the sea and preyed on passing ships. Never had they rushed back asking them to follow them down to the cove. Alegria and her husband looked up from their crab chowder in concern and alarm.

"What is it?" spoke her father Agrio, his mouth still crammed with the crumbs of fresh-baked laver bread.

"Someone's lying on the beach. They're not moving."

"What have we told you, girls, about being dishonest?"

"Exactly what I've told you about eating with your mouth full!" returned Alegria playfully, making a swipe at her husband with a tea cloth while standing and brushing down her skirts. She turned to the youngest of the two, who they had named Ocarina.

"What have you seen?"

"There's a lady on the beach, just down between the place where the lobster pots sit and the stone arch at the end of the cove," she said, getting her breath back now. "Oh please, mama, papa, come see! She's been washed up from the sea and she's just lying there and not moving." Her freckled, sun-dappled face looked up pleadingly, into her mother's eyes. "I think she's dead. I don't know who she is but there must be people that are missing her, mustn't there mama?"

"We should go look." Alegria looked over at Agrio who was wiping the last of the stew and breadcrumbs from his mouth.

"It will be another fanciful tale!" Agrio replied, putting his napkin down. "An errand for a fool. Come, let us drink this fine wine your sister brought on her last trip and then go into the square for the dancing. There will be plenty more stories where that came from, let me tell you!"

Alegria shot a glance at Agrio that would have killed a shark stone-dead in the water.

"I will come with you, Ocarina. You and Serena can lead me to her. Let us leave your father here to his wine and his pipe while we go on a little adventure." She was often dragged out of their hut by young Ocarina, whose eyes were always wide with wonder and whose feet were fleet and sure as a mountain goat. Often, she clambered over the stones and rocks at the end of the cove and left her breathless halfway down the beach.

But not today.

"I'll show you the way! Come, mamma!" Alegria took her outstretched hand and was led outside where the vibrant reds of the sunset, the golden sands of the beach and the pearly-white of the full, low moon took her breath away every time she saw them together. Serena followed slowly behind them, ever at her own dreamy pace, silent and withdrawn. Alegria often wondered what was going on behind those misty grey eyes.

As they crossed the crest of the little hill, Alegria surveyed the whole beach below them, squinting against the darkness to see what the fuss was, and drew a sharp intake of breath. Strewn out along the curve of the cove was the wreck of a huge ship - bigger than any that could berth in their little harbour - three masts at least. It was clear from the pattern of the wreckage that it hadn't been driven by the storm to beach here but had encountered the full strength of the tempest while still on the high sea whereupon the winds and currents had carried the debris to their little stretch of the coast. She said a quick prayer for the souls the storm had taken, then remembered that there was at least one who they might still be able to save, one who might even have answers.

Alegria gathered her skirts and ran over to where the woman was sprawled on the beach with the waves gently lapping at her feet and long strands of kelp matted in her auburn hair. It only took one look to realise there was little chance of her having survived. She took a pulse anyway, more out of instinct than of hope. As she squatted on the soft sand, a long shadow was cast over her.

"Is this how you found us?" Serena rarely spoke, but when she did it was invariably a question. Neither of their girls had ever asked about that day before. Alegria looked up at her daughter, a small tear welling at the corner of her eye. Serena looked down at her mother, her face cocked at an odd angle which made her look less human somehow. Her straight blond hair was tied tidily back in a bun and her face, despite the amount of sun that graced their bay, somehow remained forever pale.

"No, not like this. You were awake and sitting on a sea-chest when we found you, reading a book. Ocarina was running round on the beach in circles kicking up patches of sand." As she spoke, Ocarina came into view, her arms full of what looked like charts.

"I found these! Look! They're all maps of the sea. I bet there's treasure marked on them, like in the stories!" Ocarina's eyes - in contrast to the droopy, half-closed lids of her sister, were always wide open and fascinated at every sight and movement. Sometimes Alegria and her husband struggled to keep up with her constant prattle, good-natured though it was. She looked up at her daughter, her eyes twinkling but wrinkled at the corners in lines of crow's feet that extended nearly to the salt-and-pepper hairline in front of her ears. The sun over Esperanza was not always kind to the complexion, but it was kinder than the ocean.

"What have you got there, little one?" Alegria was interested, but also concerned. How much else had washed up here? Would they be able to collect it all before the rest of the townsfolk laid claim? The local laws specified a 'finders, keepers' attitude when it came to claiming property from ships that foundered off the coast, as long as there were no survivors. The trouble was that the arm of the law was only as long as the council wished it to be. Since they inhabited the closest hut to the bay where ships most often run aground, there had been murmurs and evil stirrings among the others, even though they shared everything they found. Agrio had nearly gotten into a knife fight only three

67

moons ago: it had taken a collective effort to talk both parties down.

Ocarina dropped the bundles of charts unceremoniously just above the tide line and the two of them began to inspect them. Serena took one look and then - seemingly uninterested - yawned and sat down on a nearby rock. She tugged at the binding on her bun and shook her hair free, then started brushing it. She let her feet dangle in the warm evening waters, staring out over the bay and only occasionally casting a glance back at her sister and mother. Whatever she was thinking, she chose - as usual - not to share it. When the girls were younger, this had concerned their adopted parents but now they just accepted that Serena liked her quiet time. They usually had their hands full with Ocarina anyway. Currently, Alegria was very occupied with what Ocarina had found, with what else might be on the beach and then, suddenly, by the fact that the woman they thought was dead had suddenly sat bolt upright and began gasping and coughing.

***

"We need to talk about your girls."

Agrio had grown impatient waiting for his wife and children to return from what was almost certainly a fool's errand. Instead, he had poured a large draught of spiced wine into a clay jug and wandered half-drunk into the village square to watch the dancing. He hadn't expected Barzao to be there, not this early, so the confrontation took him a little off-guard.

"Oh, aye?" Agrio raised a bushy eyebrow at Barzao, who stood over the seated Agrio intrusively, his arms folded and his long shadow leaving Agrio in a sliver of darkness even though the town plaza was lit by a hundred burning torches. "What have they done now?" Agrio was willing to contemplate that the tempestuous Ocarina had made some offhand remark which had roused Barzao's temper - that was hardly difficult for anyone to do - but somehow, he expected this was different.

"Saw they were down in the next bay again, soon as the storm abated."

"No law against them playing in the bay." Agrio tensed. He didn't like where he suspected this was heading.

"Was that what they were doing? Looks to me like they were making sure you got the pick of the spoils." Barzao hadn't moved his feet, not even a shuffle, but now he folded his muscled arms across his chest. Agrio wished he was standing up - he was taller than Barzao if not wider - and that he hadn't had quite as much wine.

"You know they have a secret cave up by the north cliffs? I've seen them clambering up there when I've been out fishing... He patted the lid of his satchel from which protruded a well-fashioned spyglass. Agrio decided not to mention to Barzao that his spyglass had also been claimed flotsam once. He was too busy being both annoyed and curious that apparently his daughters had a secret treasure trove they'd decided not to share knowledge of with their adopted father.

"No, I didn't know that. Full of kids' stuff, I expect. Odd-shaped stones, strings of that glowy seaweed that washes up sometimes..."

Barzao looked long and hard at Agrio, trying to decide if he was bluffing, Evidently, he thought he wasn't.

"What did they find this time? Anything you care to share?" Agrio shrugged.

"Does it matter? Finders' keepers, that's what the town law says. Not my fault if you can't haul your lazy ass over to the next beach as soon as the weather settles." That was a mistake, he knew that as soon as it left his lips. Barzao went redder than summer wine.

"Some of us were busy checking the buildings in the town," He jerked his thumb back to where a couple were picking through their goods outside a dilapidated shack. "And those repairs are going to be costly this time. We could do with more to sell at the inland market to pay for them."

"You think we make a fortune from what washes up?" It was Agrio's turn to become inflamed. He even stood in defiance, without even realising it. "Mostly it's garbage, A few good timbers, the odd crate of cargo. Mostly we hand it over to the council to sell anyway. What's left pays for our own upkeep.

"That's not all you kept though, is it?"

Agrio looked perplexed for a moment. He wasn't sure what Barzao was suggesting.

"Those two girls of yours."

Agrio balled his hands into fists.

"What about them? They're a blessing to us, is what they are. Not a day goes past when we don't count those two blessings as the best thing the sea ever gave up to us."

"I want to see that cave, Agrio, and I'm not going to take no for an answer. I can't believe you don't know about it. If I find out you've been holding back more than your due, then by the currents I'll…"

Agrio raised his hand. "Point taken," He lowered his face dejectedly. "I'll see what I can do."

"See what you can do? They're only small children."

"They're more than that." Agrio muttered under his breath. "They're blessings." He slunk off back home before Barzao decided to insist on going immediately.

***

"We've got trouble, Alegria."

"Oh, and where have you been? Wait, don't tell me, I know. Drunk in the village square. Well don't think I…"

"I mean it."

Alegria gave some serious side-eye. Ordinarily, she might have let him continue, but she had news herself.

"This is Lucia." Alegria pointed over to their cot in the corner. "We found her on the beach, nearly dead. Remember?"

So, it had been true. He should never have doubted.

"Does anyone else know she's here?"

Alegria looked her husband up and down quickly. That was such an unusual thing for him to say that she decided to let him continue.

"They say we take the best of the flotsam. That we don't give them enough."

"And who's they, as if I didn't know? Well, they're welcome to argue the point. We know it's not true."

"I think it's beyond arguing. Apparently, the girls have a little cave up in the cliffs where they've been hiding flotsam. Barzao is insisting we take him there - soon - and he's not going to take no for an answer."

Alegria looked alarmed at this. *So, she doesn't know either. That's something.* Whatever trust he had lost in his wife's judgement was doubly restored.

"Am I going to be a burden?" A raspy voice from the cot in the corner reminded them they still had a visitor. "I couldn't help overhearing. I can guess your local custom, they're pretty much the same up and down the coast. I can arrange a message to someone…" Lucia struggled to stand, then slumped back. Alegria took hold of Agrio's arm and led him outside. "I'll stay here and take care of her. They won't be able to claim anything from today's catch" - she gestured at a wheelbarrow full of oddities - "If there's still a survivor with a valid claim on part of the cargo. Those are the rules, as Barzao knows well."

"Oh Alegria, I think he's beyond the rules now…"

"Been scuffling and squabbling again? You and your tongue, you've really got us into trouble this time haven't you!" Her tone began as a scold but grew into a concern. She looked around. "Where are the girls now? They were here a few minutes ago."

"You don't think..."

"That's exactly what I think. You'd better get up there sharpish and deal with Barzao any way you can. Negotiate if you need to. Appease him with a few trinkets, because otherwise..."

"I know, I know. Why just take the treasures when you can make a claim to the treasure makers? The law isn't clear on the ownership of people, not really, because it's always been obvious that people can't be owned. But it is pretty clear on flotsam. That's the angle he'll use, assuming he doesn't come straight in with bared chest and bruised knuckles."

"I'll go now. I'm faster than him. If he's not ahead of us already, I'll find the girls and make sure they're safe. I won't let them take the girls away from us. The rest is, as you say, negotiable."

Agrio sped off over the little hillock toward the cove.

***

Ocarina had heard her parents arguing and bolted while they were distracted. She wasn't sure she understood everything, but she understood enough - especially where their secret cave was concerned. She raced along the beach, darting at speed between the smooth, slippery stones which dotted the beach at the low tide mark and the fierce jagged rocks which marked the extent of the ocean's

73

domain at high tide. Her sister was nowhere to be seen, as usual, but she assumed she was somewhere behind her. Serena was never too far behind. She'd never be the one to get into trouble herself, but she always helped her little sister out when it was needed.

She began scrabbling up the cliff. The handholds were a little too far apart for her so there were some perilous moments where she nearly lost her balance. Her right food was bleeding where she had brushed it against a rugged outcrop and the blood made her foot slipperier than usual. Of course, that did nothing to dissuade her, not when they were about to be discovered. She still couldn't see Serena, but she did make out a figure in a bright red shirt making headway across the beach. It wasn't her father, she knew that, so she assumed it was the man who was trying to lay claim to their little world. She balled her hands up into little fists in defiance for a moment, then wiped sweat away from her forehead and concentrated on the cliff.

Behind her, Barzao was gaining ground rapidly on her. She knew it wouldn't be long until he reached the cliff and he'd find it easier to climb than she did, even if she did know all the best places to put her hands and feet and the two spaces where you had to jump. She daren't look back now.

***

Even further behind, Agrio was puffing his breathless way across the cove, following Barzao's footprints in the sand when he lost sight of the red shirt among the rocks. He was beginning to realise he might be too late.

Barzao reached the base of the cliff and began to look for the best way to ascend. As he looked up, a rock struck him squarely on the forehead, scattering dust into his eyes.

"Why, you little..."

Ocarina looked down to see what had happened. She hadn't meant to dislodge the stone, she'd just slipped, and it had dislodged itself from the cliff to join the scree at the bottom. It did give her an idea though. When she reached the next place she could rest, she gathered up a handful of pebbles and put them in her apron pocket.

Barzao shrieked in agony when the next stone struck. He instinctively tried to shield himself with a broad forearm, but that was problematic when you needed both hands to climb. So, he endured a barrage of increasingly larger rocks, each time cursing Ocarina above.

Ocarina reached the next platform, very close to the lip of the cave. This was the last place she had to jump carefully to another part of the cliff face. Even her sister had to jump. She didn't know if the man would too or whether he was tall enough to step over. None but she and her sister had been her before. Where was her sister, anyway? She looked down and around for any sign of her and distracted herself for one second too long. "Got you now, you little menace!" A powerful hand took hold of her ankle and she tried to kick it away. As she did, she could feel herself losing her balance.

"Noooo!" Agrio reached the bottom of the cliff just in time to see Ocarina begin to flail and scream as she plummeted from the cliff face. He did not have time to catch her before she landed at the bottom of the cliff. Her body shuddered for a moment, then laid perfectly still. A few moments later, as Agrio held his head in his hands, it was borne away by a wave and carried away by the pull of the tide.

Even Barzao watched in horror at what happened. But that didn't deter him for more than a few moments, not when the prize was so close! One stretch of his long legs was all it would take to cross the gap between the rocks and then he would be just below the lip of the cave itself. He began thinking again of what treasures lay within. As he drew himself upward to the shelf, he imagined chests of gold coins and jewels that would make him the richest and most powerful man on the coast. What he didn't expect to see was Serena waiting for him there with a large piece of driftwood aimed square at his face.

Seconds later, he also fell. Agrio watched as his body went limp and then just laid still on the stones. He looked up to see what had happened but did not see his other daughter. It would be some time before he did. He shook his head, tears running down his cheeks, as he returned to Alegria to tell her the bad news. He had quite forgotten about the cave. No amount of treasure could make up for the treasure they had lost.

***

Later that evening, Serena sat on the rocks out by the cliffs at the north end of the bay, alone and silent. Then, from behind her back, she drew forth the conch she had picked up in the cave and put it to her lips. The shell did nothing at first, but then quivered, resonated, and brought forth a cacophony of torrents barely audible to human ears. Deep in the ocean, though, ears heard it and knew what it meant. A great power of currents gathered and gave birth to waves taller than any shack in Esperanza. The skies answered too; great dark clouds gathered on the horizon and began rolling in, lashing sheets of light against the dark waters. All the sea was angry at that point, an anger and a passion that would soon be unleashed on the land.

Until then, Serena sat alone on the rocks, looking out to sea, and brushing her hair. The calm before the storm.

Steel Velvet
(Rie Sheridan Rose)

Carter Dallas tested off the scale on most IQ batteries, but unlike the stereotypical "egghead," he had twenty-twenty vision and a love for sports that had earned him three letters in high school. Upon graduation from MIT, every think tank in the country—not to mention a few abroad, and the one on Moon Alpha—tried to wine and dine him before he chose private research instead. He helped to create the Sigma Five Database, which catapulted storage and retrieval systems into the next level. Not to mention the fact his work with navitronics had opened a real possibility of colonization to the World Space Consortium. However, all his spare time went into a private endeavor: laboring to create the ideal woman…

He built his first android at eight—and had spent the next twenty-five years working to perfect her. As he grew older, the chassis changed to reflect a developing awareness of form and function. Proportions expanded alarmingly when he was about fourteen and shrank to more aesthetically pleasing levels in his mid-twenties. After his thirtieth birthday, her body remained constant, but her face was ever-changing.

When he was a kid, he called her "Ann Droid," snickering with his friends over the joke, but as he grew older, he called her "Galatea"—and kept the conceit private. He strove for an unattainable perfection, a modern-day Pygmalion without the safety net of divine guidance.

Of late, the quest had taken on a more frenetic pace. At his yearly physical, Carter had learned it would probably be his last. Something about a rare blood disorder...chemical imbalance...he didn't really know—medical science had simply never interested him, to his mother's abiding disappointment. All he knew was the meter was running, and he wanted to finish his creation—to leave one thing of beauty behind him when he went.

It got harder to concentrate for long periods of time, and he often dropped things—his hands simply losing strength in mid-task. He'd given up his softball league already...and the weekly racquetball match with his best friend, Jerry. He'd even given up the beach house and moved into his studio laboratory to be closer to his work. He was wrapping things up, like a Going-out-of-Business Sale, terrified it was already too late.

It was well past two in the morning. The phone trilled, but he ignored it, knowing the record-call would automatically log it in and knowing the odds were ten to one, it was just his mother's daily worry call. She tried odd times, hoping to catch him unawares, but he was wise to her ways. When he had moved here from the beach house, he hadn't transferred the vid-phone because he didn't want her to see how far the disease had gone and worry even further. So far, he had stalled her from visiting by pleading a deadline—but the excuse was wearing thin. He dreaded the day he could no longer put off that goodbye....

He was puttering around Galatea, adjusting a screw here, replacing a fitting there, resettling a spun filament curl just so against her bare shoulder. The golden metal gleamed with a burnished sheen, like steel velvet, and he half-expected it to be soft and warm beneath his questing fingertips, but the shining skin was cold.

"If only you could talk to me," he sighed, running the back of his hand down Galatea's cool, golden cheek.

Her eyes whirred open. She looked at him. "What do you wish me to say?"

He retreated a step in shock; his own eyes captured by the violet lights of hers. "You can talk."

"Yes."

"But I didn't program you to talk! Your circuits aren't even capable of that function. I need a new ROM chip, and a voice synthesizer, and—"

"Do you not wish me to talk?" she asked, as her head cocked in an android equivalent of a puzzled frown.

"Of course I do...but it isn't scientifically possible!"

"Ah...then I will remain silent until it is." Her face seemed to freeze, and the light in her eyes dimmed a little.

"No! Wait! Please...I'd like you to talk to me...I've waited so long," he whispered.

Her eyes brightened once more. "And I, too, have waited, Carter Dallas. For twenty-five years I have waited—until you should ask me to speak."

"I was just a kid then."

"Yes, with a child's sense of beauty." Her voice deepened with amusement. "Luckily, you outgrew it." She lifted a graceful golden hand, joints rippling as she touched her own face. "This body and these features are very pleasing to me."

"I'm glad you approve, Gal—wait, what should I call you?"

"I have no quarrel with Galatea."

"But what's your name*? That's just what I stuck you with."*

"It suits me better than 'Ann Droid.' Do you not think so?"

The reminder brought a hectic flush to his pale cheek. "I'm sorry about that."

"It is of no concern. May I sit?"

"Oh, geez...yes, of course! I've had you standing for twenty-five years! I'm so sorry. Please, sit here." He led her to the stuffed armchair that was the most comfortable seat in the cluttered one-room apartment.

She folded easily to sit in the chair.

He only then realized her nudity. It had never come to mind when she was an inanimate android—sort of a moving statue—but now.... His blush deepened.

"Would you like a...robe or something?" he mumbled.

"Why? Is this body no longer pleasing to you?"

"No...I mean yes! Yes, it's very pleasing. I just thought you...might be uncomfortable."

"My functions are all satisfactory, thank you."

81

Carter sank down on the hassock at her feet. "I still can't believe you're real."

"But you built me."

"Yeah, I built you...but I surely didn't make you like this...."

"Oh, but you did."

"I don't have the skill."

"But you have the heart. Do you not see that?"

"What do you mean?" Carter asked, his confusion growing, along with his fatigue.

"It is late, Carter Dallas. You are tired. You must rest now. We will talk more in the morning. If you do not sleep, you will weaken more quickly, and you may not finish your work."

"What is there to finish?" he mumbled fuzzily. "You're perfect...." His head fell back onto the arm of the chair, and he slid into sleep. Galatea picked him up as if he were a child and carried him to the daybed in the corner.

She settled him on the bed and pulled an afghan over him. Brushing the sandy hair from his forehead, she whispered, "Rest well, Carter Dallas. You have earned it."

Galatea sat at his bedside for the remainder of the night, eyes dimly glowing as internal gears whirred softly....

Carter awoke the next morning refreshed, but sure the conversation of the night before had been merely a work-induced dream. Galatea stood in her customary spot. With her magnificent eyes closed, she posed just as he had left her at the end of the workday. He sighed and sat up on the edge of the bed, shaking his head at his fancies.

Her eyes whirred open and charged to full glow. "Good morning, Carter Dallas," she greeted him.

"You're real," he breathed.

"Yes."

"I thought I'd dreamed you."

"No. I am as I am."

He tried to stand, only to fall back onto the bed. Galatea was at his side in an instant, a supporting hand under his arm.

"I'm getting worse, aren't I?"

"Yes, Carter Dallas. You have not much time."

He raised a trembling hand to stroke her cool metal cheek. "My sense of timing has always been horrible, hasn't it?"

"I do not understand you."

"Never mind. What will happen to you when I...when I'm...gone?"

"What do you mean?"

"Where will you go?"

"That is your decision. You are my creator."

"I can't send you somewhere where they'd take you apart...or experiment on you. I couldn't bear that."

"The time is not yet here. Do not worry about it today. Come." She helped him to the small counter that doubled as a kitchen table and workbench and made him eat something. He never took his eyes off her.

Carter picked up a small circuit board from the clutter on the table, fiddling with it absently.

"Something troubles you, Carter Dallas?"

"Yeah," he sighed. "I just wish...I wish I could stay here with you." He met her eye squarely. "Now I've finally got you; I don't want to let go. I don't think I ever really expected to finish...I certainly didn't expect this!"

"We have a little time. We must make the best of it."

"I just wish...."

"Wish what?"

He flushed. "That there was a way to make it last forever."

"Forever is a long time, Carter Dallas."

"It's not long enough."

"What would you do with forever? Where would you go?"

His eyes lit up. "The stars. Just think...if you could live forever, you could explore the galaxies. Find those worlds to colonize—I know they're out there...but no human being can survive long enough to find them with our present technology. But you could..." he continued thoughtfully. "If you went out on an Explorer, no one would ever hurt you."

"I cannot be hurt, only disassembled."

"I don't believe that. There is more to you than that. Perhaps it once was true, but something wonderful has happened. You are a unique creature."

"It is kind of you to say so." Her mouth quirked in a little smile. At least...it seemed to him as if she smiled. It must be a trick of the light or a blurring of his vision. How could she possibly smile? Her face was lovely, but with all the articulation of marble. A

84

*cool metal representation of an ideal—like a mask.
She was incapable of expression. And yet...she* had
smiled. He knew it in his heart.

*"Would you really like to journey the stars for
eternity, Carter Dallas?"*

"I would if it were with you."

"You would tire of me after a century or so."

"Never."

*"How would you occupy your mind without
your laboratory and equipment?"*

*"If I had a computer...and enough storage
space...I could do the theoretical work and dock
every hundred years or so to do the applications—"*

She laughed. "You have *thought this all out,
have you not?"*

*"Just think—" he continued eagerly, as he
warmed to his subject. "Soon they will have
colonies ready to begin settlement. As man moves
out into the universe, there will be chances to build
and work on other planets, around other suns. It
will be awe-inspiring."*

*"How badly do you wish it, Carter Dallas?"
Her voice hummed with intensity—literally
vibrating in her throat.*

*"More than life," he replied earnestly. "As long
as I would have you beside me, I'd do anything you
say."*

"There is a way."

"What do you mean?"

"If you wish it badly enough, Carter Dallas."

"What would I have to do?"

"Kiss me."

He blinked in surprise—but then wondered why. Why else had he been building her but as an embodiment of desire? If she had come to life, why should she not want the trappings of romance? Would it not be part of her "function?"

He bent forward, eyes closing in anticipation, and pressed his lips to hers. He expected cool, hard metal, but her mouth was surprisingly giving. A sensation like a current rippled between them...swirling emotions and impressions of things he didn't fully understand—heavy, dark, metallic images....

He felt a shifting somewhere deep inside of him, and pulled away with a start, his eyes flying open. "What just happened?"

His senses expanded to enfold a thousand nuances he had never experienced before. His sight sharpened to a clarity inhumanly possible. He held his hand before his face and watched his skin tighten and smooth, the pore definition melting into a shining golden surface that matched Galatea's perfection.

His breath caught in his chest in wonder, and the exhale never came. He laid his new hand on his chest and felt no heartbeat. He had never felt more alive, and yet....

"Am I dead?" he whispered.

"Welcome to a brave new world, Carter Dallas."

***

The transport team from Galaxy Five Deep Space Probe let themselves in with a passkey obtained from Carter's mother. The apartment was

86

neat, except for a fine film of dust shrouding the furniture. "That must be what we're supposed to pick up," said one tech, pointing at a group of boxes in the center of the floor.

"Yeah," answered the second tech, consulting his clipboard, "two wooden crates—Handle with Care, no less—and a box of computer equipment."

His partner circled the crates curiously. "Wonder what's in 'em?"

"Beats me. Let's move 'em out. I've got this one," he grunted, slipping a dolly under the crate marked GALATEA. "You bring that one," he ordered, jerking his head at the crate labeled PYGMALION.

Death in the Dust
(Rie Sheridan Rose)

"There's a body outside Airlock Two."

"Bloody hell. What happened this time? Bad suit?"

"No suit. Stark bollocks naked."

"Outstanding." Director Caruthers sighed heavily, shoved his chair back from his desk, and offered his full attention to his visitor. *What the hell was going on around here these days? Whatever had possessed him to come to the moon...?* "Some kid on a dare? Damn twenty-nine second morons. Awful lot of faith to put in a stopwatch."

"You wouldn't catch me doing it. Not for a million credits." Officer Parsons shook his head. "But no, no kid this time. Looks like one of the business people from Dome Nine."

Caruthers closed his eyes and counted to ten. *Some days it doesn't pay to get out of bed in the artificial morning.* "Take a crew and bring the body inside. Get him to Doc Harris as soon as possible. I need to know if there is any evidence of foul play."

"Oh, yeah. There is," Parsons replied without moving to obey.

"What?"

"They found his head sitting in the middle of his back, grinning at the airlock."

"Be-au-ti-ful." Caruthers ran his hands through what little hair he had left. *This job will be the death of me yet. Maybe it's time to retire...*

"Get him to the morgue. Take the back ways. We don't want anyone to see it. Wait, strike that. I should see him *in situ*. Secure the area. I'll meet you there."

"Right, Boss." Parsons turned and left the office.

Caruthers snagged his helmet and buzzed Chief Osaka on the comm. "Satsuo, meet me in the morgue. I should be there in about ten minutes. We have a situation to discuss."

"The dead guy?"

"So, you've heard."

"*Hai.*"

Jamming his helmet onto his suit, Caruthers keyed open the nearest airlock. Cutting across the exterior of the colony would save a bit of time. He stepped onto the lunar surface and glanced up at the Earth hanging overhead—a beautiful, blue-green jewel. Too bad no one sane could live on it these days. At least if you liked movement. More people inhabited it than places to put them. Boxy condo units everywhere, all jobs filled by telecommuting, and no one ever left their homes. He couldn't stand the thought of it.

Not that the moon had been his first choice. He had wanted to apply for one of the generation ships, but the cutoff for volunteers was twenty, and he had just passed his twenty-first birthday at the time.

No amount of persuasion could induce the Colonization Board to make an exception for him, so he applied to the moon-base. In the next two decades, he'd worked his way up to Base Director. Days like this, he wished he'd never left Earth.

The body was as Parsons had described it— buck naked and headless on the gray lunar dust. The head sat on the back of the corpse, face set in a rictus grin, and turned toward the porthole windows of the travel-way.

Fourteen interconnected domes set around a central command center comprised the base. Housed within those domes, ten thousand people lived, worked, and played. And, apparently, died. This made the third body to turn up in the past two months with obvious signs of foul play.

Two thousand residents remained under the age of ten. He guessed he could safely count them out of the suspect pool, at least for the moment. But that still left almost eight thousand potential murderers. Shit.

Parsons and two of his fellow officers stood beside the body. Caruthers circled the corpse. No blood, of course. Any there might have been had boiled away. The head had been cleanly severed— no hesitation to the wound. Whoever had done this was strong and determined. Though that didn't necessarily rule out the women or the teenagers. You had to be of hardy stock to emigrate to the colony.

Caruthers gestured toward the airlock, and the officers picked up the corpse and carried it into the base. They got to the morgue, attracting no unwarranted attention. Thank goodness for small favors.

Satsuo Osaka waited for them in the morgue with Doctor Sandra Harris. The Chief of Police was small and wiry, showing his Asian origins in his dark hair and sloe eyes. By contrast, the doctor towered over him at almost six feet, her blonde hair military short. Rumor made them bedmates. Not that it mattered to Caruthers.

"Put him down on the table," Harris ordered. "We've got to stop meeting like this, Gordon," she continued in her clipped accent. "I've got plenty of work on my own without these presents you keep bringing in."

"Tell me about it, Sandy," Caruthers sighed. "It's obvious what killed him. Run him through the database. Let's find out who he is." Thank God for small favors. The small-town level population of the colony made it easy for management to keep tabs on everyone. All the moon base's citizens went into the computer's voracious mainframe within hours of birth or arrival.

"Give me a moment..." She picked up the handheld unit and ran it across the corpse's hands, collecting fingerprint data. She glanced at the reading and drew in a sharp breath. "That can't be right."

With a frown of concentration, she ran the scan more slowly. Then she glanced up at Caruthers, her face white. "This is Foster Danbridge."

"I thought he looked familiar," Parsons murmured.

"Refresh my memory. Danbridge is...?"

Osaka replied, his face grim. "He's the stepson of the Governor."

"Bloody hell," Caruthers swore. "This will bite us in the ass. Satsuo—this is your top priority. We've got to figure out who killed him *yesterday*. Tell me about the other two recent murders. Is there anything which connects them?"

Osaka checked his wristcomp, tapping information into the keypad. "The first death was Carter Nelson, age twenty. He worked in the hydro-gardens of Dome Three. Found under a tree in the garden with a slit throat. Next, Harrison Green, age twenty-three. A custodian in Dome Six. They found him stuffed into the recycler unit near his supply closet with his head nearly severed."

"Hang on—" Sandra checked her own records. "Danbridge is twenty-six, and he worked in Dome Nine. Satsuo...am I crazy, or is there a pattern here?"

Osaka frowned, keying more information into his unit. "You may be on to something, Sandy...twenty/three/minor wound; twenty-three/six/nearly severed head; twenty-six/nine/decapitation. They are moving through the domes in threes, every death a man three years older, and escalating the violence of the murder. But how can you escalate from a severed head? And why these three men? How is the killer choosing his or her victims? Are they related? Are they all the same killer?"

Caruthers exhaled loudly. "Great questions. How the hell are we supposed to catch this bastard?"

"What about a set-up?" asked Parsons. "If the pattern holds, the next victim will be twenty-nine and work in Dome Twelve. Can we put out a Judas goat? Find a volunteer on the force who will make themselves a target?"

"Will it do any good until we can figure out what connects these men? This pattern is too

92

detailed. It's insane. Something caused the murderer to choose them, and if we don't match his full pattern exactly, he won't take the bait."

"What's the time between the murders? Is that part of the pattern, too?"

"Looks like three weeks exactly between incidents. Since they found Danbridge tonight—Sandy, he *was* killed tonight, wasn't he?"

"The evidence seems to bear that out."

"So, we have three weeks at most—but, hopefully, we do *have* three weeks to sort this." Caruthers ran his hands through his hair again. "Three years apart in age, three domes apart in residence, three weeks apart in death. What is this? Some kind of trinity reference...? Osaka—look for a solid connection of some kind between these three men. Sandy—figure out what killed them...weapon-wise. Parsons—talk to the men and see if you can find someone on the force who fits the pattern of victims—just in case three isn't enough for him. We've got to stop this crazy. Now, let's get to work."

By dinnertime, Sandra Harris had determined the same sharp weapon murdered all three men—apparently some sort of sword. Caruthers stared at the report in his hand. *Bloody hell, who keeps a* sword *in these enlightened times?*

Some heirloom, he supposed. Who might have an heirloom like that? Japanese emigrants like Osaka—in fact, he could remember seeing a matched set of ceremonial samurai swords in Satsuo's quarters. Maybe the Chief could talk to his compatriots.

There might also be a few claymores from the Highlands…but swinging one of those in low-grav might be problematic. Assuming the murderer killed Danbridge where they found him, and not inside the base…killing him inside would have presented its own problems.

Who else might have a sword? He should have put that into the database. They tracked the projectile weapons, but never thought of logging the exotic weapons. He'd have to send someone door-to-door, he supposed.

Caruthers made a note.

***

Two weeks later, Caruthers was ready to pull what remained of his hair out of his head.

Osaka had wracked his brains nearly to the bursting point, but he still couldn't determine any relationship between the three dead men. As the pattern date neared, Caruthers was worried they might not catch the bastard before he could commit another murder.

He keyed the comm to Parsons. "Steve—have you come up with a volunteer for next Thursday?"

"Not yet, boss. No one on the force quite meets those specifications."

Caruthers allowed himself a sigh. Bloody hell, not one single man on the force was twenty-nine years old? That seemed unlikely.

"Keep trying," he ordered, turning back to his own copies of the crime scene reports. Something here *had* to break the case. Carter Nelson, Harrison Green, Foster Danbridge. Three young men with seemingly nothing in common. They hailed from different social strata, they worked in different parts of the base, and yet…a niggling itch at the back of his brain said he was missing something here.

Wait a minute…

Not a lot of crime happened on the base. Most days, administrating this place felt like a walk in the park…probably why he had stuck it out so long.

But a couple of Earth months back, there had been an incident…a child…what were the details? A young girl found beaten and terrified. Three young men accused but acquitted for lack of evidence. There must be a file here somewhere…

He found the report he was looking for and spread the pages in front of him in a fan. "Hang on a minute…"

He frowned, bending closer to the papers, and scanning down them with his finger. "Holy hell."

He leaned back in his chair. Now it all made sense. He keyed the comm, "Parsons. I need you. Now."

"On my way." Steve Parsons was a good officer. Methodical, precise, and really caring for the position, he wanted to make the police force his life. This might test that decision.

Caruthers checked his findings again. He saw little chance of mistake.

Parsons knocked on the doorframe. "You wanted to see me, boss?"

"Come in and shut the door."

The young officer did as his commander requested.

"Have a look at this and tell me what you see." Caruthers pushed the incident report across the desk, and Parsons sank into the chair opposite. He scanned down the pages as Caruthers had done.

Caruthers saw the precise moment it hit him. Parsons started like a racehorse struck by a crop. "Oh, my God…"

"She was nine. I don't know how we missed this earlier. It's right there in black and white. We were looking for a connection, but we had the wrong man searching. How did this slip past me?" He ran a hand over his face. "I'm really too old for this job."

"Don't be silly, boss. It's easy to miss. They anglicized her name here. Here it's in kanji. Here it's romanized. Still…I should have thought of it…double-checked the chief. I'll turn in my badge if you need it."

"No reason you should have thought of that. With Sandra backing him up, they could easily manipulate the investigation. Bringing up the pattern…never mind—I just checked. Harrison Green was thirty. The whole pattern was a lie, but no one checked the data.

"Satsuo and Sandra were beyond reproach. Sloppy of me." Caruthers held up a hand. "No, Steve—if anything, you'll get a promotion out of this. I'll need someone I can trust in that position…after. Shall we get it over with?"

Parsons nodded grimly.

***

He met them at the door. "I've been expecting you." Osaka stepped back from the opening. "Come in, please."

They followed the Chief into his living quarters. Huddled in one corner of the seating unit sat a tiny girl bundled into a heavy quilted coat, despite the fact the quarters felt rather over-heated. "This is my daughter, Aiko—Alice in the formal records." He stroked her hair, and she shrank back against the cushions of the sofa. "She's all I have left since her mother died. She hasn't been out of the house since that night."

"What happened, Satsuo?"

"She and her friends played too long in the hydro-garden. It was time for her to come home, and she was hurrying because she was going to be late for curfew…they stopped her just inside Dome Six as she cut through. Green let them into the custodian's office, and they…well, you can guess. Then they forced her out of airlock two and ran. Thank God, someone was passing through the travel-way and saw her out there before it was too late. They brought her home…

"She recognized all of them from their citizen ids…but the Governor hushed things up. She thought she could buy me off. I took her money to give Aiko a chance at a future. But I made sure those bastards got what they deserved."

"You know we have to take you in, Satsuo," Caruthers murmured with a frown.

"*Hai*. Aiko goes back to Japan on the next shuttle to live with my sister. I hope she will come back to life, eventually."

"I understand your reasons, Satsuo. I do. But I have to—"

97

"I know." Osaka held out his wrists. "Parsons, I am ready." He glanced over at Caruthers. "May Aiko stay with Sandra until the shuttle comes?"

"I'm afraid that won't be possible. Sandra had a part in this, too."

"Will you take her, then?"

The question startled Caruthers. He had no experience with children...still, the next shuttle was only two days away. He could do this.

"Of course." It was the least he could do for his friend.

Osaka said something to his daughter in Japanese, and she stood, shyly shuffling to Caruthers, and holding out a tentative hand.

All of this because three young men couldn't keep their hands off a child. Maybe he should return to Earth, too. He could resign, take the child to her aunt, find himself something new to do. Right this moment, a faceless cubicle in a nameless condo block sounded like a really good idea.

Parsons led Osaka away, and Caruthers scooped Aiko into his arms. "Everything will be all right, Aiko," he murmured to the child.

Maybe he'd move to Japan.

Home By Sunset
(Rie Sheridan Rose)

The church bell sent out solemn pulses of sound, warning the citizenry to hurry behind stout doors and barred windows. A sense of urgency permeated the air as flying hooves beat a tattoo on the hard-packed surface of the lonely road leading into the secluded hamlet.

Home by sunset...must be home by sunset.

"Come on. Come on!" urged the rider, leaning low in the saddle and willing the stallion to go faster. Steel shoes struck sparks from bits of flint scattered in the roadbed. The sun sank inexorably toward the horizon, and the road seemed to stretch on forever.

Home by sunset....

The door of the barn gaped in open invitation as the rider turned into the final length of the journey. "That's it, Firemane. We're almost home. Just a little farther." Glancing over one hunched shoulder, the rider saw the disk of the sun was three-quarters below the horizon. "Come on!"

The stallion skittered to a stop inside the safety of the barn, hooves dancing as it came to a halt just as the rim of the sun disk slipped from sight. Sliding from the stallion's back, the slim rider dashed to bolt the heavy door and leaned against its shield with a gusty sigh of relief. The rider reached for the bill of a dust-covered cap.

"Katherine!" snapped a voice from the hold's inner doorway.

The rider whirled, hair fanning out in an ebony cloud as it came free of its confinement. Her breath froze in her throat, choking on her prepared excuse at the sight of her father's angry face.

"Do you realize how close that was, Kate? What would you have done if sunset caught you out? I couldn't have kept the door open—not even for you."

Katherine hung her head. "I know, Father. Forgive me. I didn't think—"

"Of course, you didn't. You never do."

Katherine loosened the girth of Firemane's saddle. "I knew we would make it," she muttered sullenly, flipping the saddle off the stallion's back and carrying it to its post.

"You were within a nail's breadth of being locked outdoors for the night, my girl. Even if you had somehow evaded the Wraiths yourself—what about Firemane?"

"No one will ever take Firemane from me. Will they, boy?" She stroked the smooth black muzzle and tugged the glowing forelock of the stallion's red-gold fiber optic mane before opening the neck panel and affixing the power cord to the horse's recharger.

"And what if they did, Katherine? Do you realize how valuable the creature is? That technology is irreplaceable out here in the colonies. I knew it was a mistake to let you accept. I don't know what your Name Father was thinking to give him to you."

"He didn't know about the Power Wraiths. No one knew." She ran a curry comb through the

100

stallion's mane and tail, then checked each steel hoof for embedded rocks or scratches.

Her father caught her shoulder and spun her to face him. "But now we do, Katherine. That automaton is a danger to the entire village."

"No, he's not!" Katherine pointed to the stout wooden door, with its inner shield of refraction alloy. "There's no power signature leak through the door. I've checked. You know the Wraiths never appear in the sunlight, so as long as we make it home before sunset, he is perfectly safe."

"It is too dangerous a risk. I have had an offer of 1,000,000 ergcreds for him. It will be your dowry. Jaston Marsh has offered suit for your hand. Perhaps he can tame that wild spirit of yours. The automaton goes tomorrow."

Katherine stared at her father, one hand resting against the warm metal musculature of the horse. "You can't do that," she whispered. "He isn't yours to sell."

"You are part of my house. What is yours is mine. When you become Jaston's wife, he will take control of you. That is the colony law."

"Firemane is *mine*! Uncle Antoine gave him to *me*!" Throat tight, she could barely breathe for the injustice of it.

Why was I born a girl? I might as well be a slave! Well, I will not stand for it. I will not*!*

Her father gave her shoulder an awkward pat, as if trying to soften the pain of the blow. "I tell you what. You can use some of the ergcreds to purchase a robotic dog...or maybe a cat—you know how you love cats. There is far less risk with a power signature of that size. And I am sure Jaston will let you choose whatever color you like."

Katherine stiffened under his hand. "Firemane is mine," she repeated through clenched teeth. "I would rather take my chances with the wraiths than stay here and marry that insipid little fool!"

She yanked the power cord out of its socket and slammed shut the panel on Firemane's neck. Before her father processed what she was doing, she threw back the bolt on the stable door and let it swing slowly inward. By the time it opened enough for passage, she had swung up on the automaton's bare back. Fingers twisted tightly in the fibers of his mane, she shouted a command, and Firemane thundered out into the night.

The last lingering traces of twilight faded around her as the stallion's steel hooves struck sparks from the flints of the road. Her heart was pounding in rhythm with the galloping tattoo.

Where will I go? I cannot stay out in the open— the power wraiths...

Her mind skittered away from the thought...but she had learned her history lessons well, and the cadence of the hoofbeats drove them through her mind.

When the ship first landed on Alteron IV two generations ago, the colonists felt they had found paradise. This climate proved perfect for growing crops. Seeds put into the ground seemed to spring up overnight. They had even considered bringing in a second ship of settlers. And then the trouble began.

102

As our village grew, the technology level rose. Ten years ago, when the power signatures reached a certain level, the power wraiths descended. Amorphous shapes, with no definable skeletal structure, which feed upon energy. I was only a little girl when they found the first victim.

The elders say the wraiths sucked the boy dry like a sun-blasted husk of corn. He collapsed in on himself, and they buried him in a foot-long box, neatly folded like a castoff sweater.

Katherine's gaze darted right and left as she flew down the deserted road. Sweat pooled inside her vest and the acid taste of fear climbed the back of her throat.

Better to die free than be forced into a loveless match.

The colonists discovered they could shield their power sources behind closed doors and barred windows. That if they could survive the nights, they could thrive in the daylight. The Power Wraiths seemed unable to face the sunlight. The elders strictly enforced a sunset curfew. Anyone caught outside the doors after sundown was on their own.

And a headstrong idiot on a 2000 megagig automaton is offering to be lunch.

She stared down the road, revealed in the light of Firemane's eyes. No sign of the creatures…but no place to hide, either. What was she to do?

She remembered when Uncle Antoine—not really an uncle, merely a Free Trader who had stood by her parents at their wedding—had given her Firemane for her seventh Name Day.

He had to pick me up and sit me on your back, didn't he, dear one? I felt as if I were on top of the world.

She bent and patted the automaton's neck. She knew he couldn't feel the affectation, but it made *her* feel better. He was real to her. More alive than some settlers she knew.

A split-second hesitation broke the smooth rhythm of Firemane's gait, and Katherine's heart skipped the next beat.

He's losing power. We rode hard today, and he didn't have time to recharge. If he stalls, I'm dead!

Again, the hesitation, and this time, the recovery took half a length.

Oh, God! He's dying!

The stallion stumbled, and Katherine gave a little gasp as he almost threw her from the saddle. The twin beams of Firemane's eyes now cast little more than moon pools, and the red-gold flames of the fiber optics that gave him his name were pale ghost fires.

A sudden tension throbbed through the air, an inaudible thrumming vibration that brought her heart into her throat.

Please, Firemane! Please! Oh, God! They're coming!

She glanced over her shoulder. The darkness shifted a little - a shadow in the shadows. They were right behind her!

She turned back to the road—and screamed, as the stallion plunged over the edge of the seaside cliff.

***

"Damn! I thought we were finally going to make contact!" Lester Cardahay stood at the edge of the cliff; his enviro-helmet tucked under one arm.

Megan Stillwell deactivated her cloaking device and stared down at the broken bodies far beneath them. "What a waste."

"I know. She couldn't have been over seventeen."

I meant the automaton." She studied the scandat device in her hand. "It possessed the largest signature we've seen since we hit this rock. Just our luck to crash into a technophobe colony. Why couldn't we have come down on Celadon V? A power source like that automaton—it might even have been enough juice to get home."

Lester threw an arm around his first mate's shoulders. "We'll get there, hun. But we've got to find some power. Too bad about the solar radiation—this sun is just a little too rich for non-enhanced blood. If we could only get hold of an enzyme hypo, we could talk to them in the daylight...."

"Ain't gonna happen, Starman. Come on. Let's check the village again. Maybe someone else got careless. After ten years, they've got to let their guard down sometime. Don't they?" Her tone sounded wistful.

Lester shrugged. "We can hope."

***

At the foot of the cliff, Firemane's eyes flickered and went out.

Ego Trip
(Marise Morland)

By day the city sleeps, its ancient stones baking in the heat of the merciless sun. But now it is twilight, and the streets will soon be alive with intrigue, laughter and danger. I attire myself, dismiss my retinue and prepare to walk amongst my subjects. My advisers have told me this is madness – that I could be courting death. But they are wrong. My people revere and fear me in equal measure, and pose no threat to me. Most dare not look upon me as I pass. Yet they know their king. How could they not?

"Albie, haven't you fixed that holocaster yet?"

"Almost done. Sand in the emitters."

"Well, sort it. We've got two strato-coaches on the way. Our tourists expect to see all the sights, not a gap where the slave market should be."

"I warned you not to book any tours for tonight. There. That should hold."

"It'd better. Now get out of the city. I'm lighting her up."

And now I am in the market-place. Fire-eaters, jesters, swordsmen, a wealth of entertainments. And further on, the slave market. I pause to inspect them: the usual assortment of thieves, foreign captives and cast-off wives. The auctioneers do not attempt to foist their wares on me. Anyone who tried would find himself enslaved on the morrow.

I dally a while longer. I have noticed a fair young girl, the last in line. She does not weep or scowl but smiles a little, eyes averted. That is pleasing. It would be unseemly for her to stare at her king.

I will buy her. I carry no coin, naturally, but will have the Keeper of the Royal Coffers make the transaction tomorrow.

I continue past stalls laden with pots and trinkets, caged birds with bright plumage, tents where passers-by may have their fortune revealed. And then, I spy her – a red-haired woman. I have never seen anything quite like her. I move to keep her in view, but she turns, confronts me boldly, and utters a challenge in a barbarian tongue. What *is* she? She is dressed as a pleasure slave but has no collar nor brand. And she is alone. A runaway, then. I step toward her; she shrieks at me and runs off.

I am enraged. She cannot escape the city as the gates are locked at night. So, I will summon the Master of the Concubines. His men will find her and bring her to me. In the meantime I shall devise a fitting punishment for her insolence.

"What do you mean, he followed her?"

Albie shuffles uncomfortably. "That's what she said. I gave her the talk about stone being a recording medium which we've learnt to scan, and that we then add continuity and sound effects..."

"I've read the brochure, Albie. Since our simulations aren't interactive it must have been another tourist stalking her."

"She knows all the tour party by sight. He wasn't one of them. And...."

"And what?"

"She said his face was like that fallen statue at our landing site. Cruel. Cold."

"I don't have time for this. Give her a refund if she won't shut up. And this – stalker – was near the slave market, you say? You need to get that system checked again. Right now."

It is day, and suddenly weary, I have returned to my palace. Is there someone I have to see before I sleep? Yes, I was to buy a slave. I need to summon…. no matter. There will always be other slaves. As for the flame-haired woman: she cannot get far in a day. When I wake, I will have my charioteers pursue her. Or perhaps I will pardon her. For am I not a benign king, a just king? Tomorrow I shall commission a statue in my likeness, and my name and deeds will live forever in this immortal city. I, Ozymandias.

Buttoned Up
(Marise Morland)

"Quantum Mechanix, policing your particles. Vooq speaking."

"Well, *don't*," the caller said irritably. "Speak, I mean. Not until you've engaged qubit encryption protocol azure."

"Azure? Do you know how much that costs?"

"Yes, and it's on us."

"It had better be. Channel is secure. What can we help you with?"

"We have a situation, Vooq. This is MIN operational headquarters. One of our buttons has malfunctioned."

Vooq uttered a startled oath.

"Naturally you're surprised to hear from us. But we've been reliably informed that your organisation can locate and reactivate the faulty button covertly and swiftly."

Vooq had every reason to be amazed. MIN, or Mutually Initiated Novae, had for aeons kept the uneasy peace between the Exfoliant Systems and the Bellicosian Cluster. The five Exfoliant buttons were linked by quantum entanglement: although they were light years apart, they would respond simultaneously and devastatingly when any of them was deployed. At least one of the buttons, according to the official story, was in neutral territory to guard against annexation.

"We can provide you with approximate locations," continued the MIN spokesman. "Approximate, because each button is hidden in plain sight and of necessity has a certain degree of mobility. But we cannot tell you which of them is defective, as each one now mirrors the defect. I am authorised to offer you a million Exfo golds, half now and half on completion of the task. You may take one assistant with you. Are the terms acceptable?"

Once again Vooq had to suppress his amazement. It was a very generous fee.

"I accept," he replied with carefully feigned indifference. "My associate Zozara will accompany me."

Quantum Mechanix had a staff of two: Vooq and his girlfriend.

"The MIN Directive is much obliged. Our downpayment will show as a credit from the Astrotrash Used Hyperdrive Warehouse. Further instructions will follow."

"These are all humanoid societies," mused Zozara, studying the newly arrived holo-map.

"Well, of course. Avians don't wear buttons. Marine life doesn't wear buttons. Saves us the trouble of hiring shifter tech. Are you ready? I don't think Mr. Min wanted us to hang about."

"You realise," said Zozara, "that they might be planning to take us out once the mission's over?"

"Don't worry. I'll sort it," Vooq assured her, though he'd no idea how.

The first button was located in a large military academy. The cadets, in endless columns, were perfecting their marching ahead of a national parade. Their double-breasted jackets had two rows of buttons. Their epaulettes, cuffs and boots also had buttons.

"I don't believe this," groaned Vooq.

"I've an idea," said Zozara. "But it means we'll have to become..." she leant forward to whisper - "fashionistas. You'll need to wear a suit. But don't worry, I'll do all the talking."

Not long afterward, she breezed confidently into the commanding officer's presence.

"Oh, were you not notified of our visit? Allow me to explain. Due to the importance of the upcoming event, we at Cosmic Couture have been appointed to provide bespoke uniforms for all your cadets. They'll look splendid! But naturally they'll need to be measured, so could you arrange for them to be scanned by my tailor? One at a time, of course! Shall we get started?"

Fortunately, the entangled button was found on the sixth cadet to be scanned. It was functioning normally.

"Let's go!" hissed Vooq.

"Sorry!" Zozara said brightly to the officer. "Change of plan. As you were."

Their second destination was a huge abbey where black-robed acolytes chanted solemnly.

"Not *another* secret society," muttered Zozara. "I suppose the button's in that casket on the altar. Are they praying to it?"

Vooq consulted his linguistic database. "No, guarding it."

The acolytes, all female, regarded them coldly. "I suppose you've come to steal the Artefact," said one.

"No, we only want to look at it," Vooq said truthfully.

"So you're pilgrims? Very well, you may approach the repository. But beware, we slay heretics." She paced toward the casket and opened it, revealing a fur-lined interior with a button nestling in its depths. The women waited, daggers drawn.

Vooq peered in, sneezed, then declared: "This is a fake."

They sheathed their daggers. "You pass the test," said their spokesperson. "You'll find the real Artefact at this address." She handed him a small scroll. Then he and Zozara were politely ejected from the abbey.

The directions on the scroll led them to a disreputable part of the city. Vooq halted in front of a shabby building. "This is it."

Zozara peered at the very small sign. "Sister Flagella's House of Correction. What does that even mean?"

"Well, it's obviously a proof-reading agency for their holy books. I've got this. Why don't you have a rest by that fountain, take the weight off? I won't be long."

Zozara was happy to do as he suggested. Presently he emerged, looking tousled.

"That was….interesting. Mind if I join you for a moment?"

"Well?" prompted Zozara when the moment was up.

"Well what? Oh, the button. No problem there. Fully functional."

112

Zozara hoped the next one would be hidden somewhere less peculiar.

It was. To be precise, it was attached to a scarecrow's threadbare overcoat. There was no-one about. The field had been harvested.

"Fully functional," announced Vooq, sounding bored.

Button number four operated a pedestrian crossing at the busiest intersection on the Exfoliant homeworld. It was, of course, fully functional.

"I knew it would be the last one," grumbled Zozara. "This is located in a non-emergent system, isn't it?"

"That's right. The planet's called Earth. Getting co-ordinates now."

Their locator took them to a street of Edwardian semis in Neasden. In the front room of one of the houses, a little girl was playing with her grandmother's sewing box.

"I'm making puddings," she announced, carefully placing one button on top of another larger one. "Yellow and blue equals blueberries and custard. Pink and green is blancmange and, um, cabbage."

"May I borrow the cabbage button?" Zozara asked sweetly. "I'll give it back in a teensy weensy – *ow!* Little brat stuck a pin in my hand."

"Then you should've let *me* talk to her," retorted Vooq. "Now look here, kid, hand the damn thing over."

"And what," said a new voice, "makes you think you can walk in here and threaten my grandchild?"

113

Vooq turned to confront the newcomer, and paled. "You're Bellicosian!"

"Quite so. I am Agent Deltress of Plethora, and I've been expecting you. Not you specifically, you understand, but whoever MIN sent. You fit the profile. Talented but missing out on big career breaks, you normally work on defective hyperdrives."

"That sounds like me," Vooq said cautiously.

"And you have little or no loyalty to the Exfoliant Alliance? You believe it to be immeasurably corrupt?"

"You said it, not me."

"Good. Now, before you inspect the bauble that Alice is so jealously guarding, I want to show you something." She rummaged in the sewing box and drew out a tarnished brass button.

Vooq readied his specialist eyepiece and examined it gingerly. "This is ruined," he said at last. "An excellent example of early quantum gothic, but irreparable. No entanglement left."

"And so it is with the remaining four of its kind," said Deltress. "The Bellicosian Cluster has had no defence for many years. I and other agents have worked ceaselessly to prevent the MIN Directive from finding out, but I fear they soon will. Alice, give him the cabbage button please."

She handed it over with a glare.

"But," said Vooq after a cursory glance, "there's nothing wrong with this. You've fitted a quantum dampener."

"To bring you here. To show you the truth and beg you not to re-arm the deterrent."

Just then, a MIN hypertransport materialised in the back yard. Two plant-based synth assassins leapt out. Deltress blasted them with a weedkiller spray and they dissolved satisfactorily. Vooq was suddenly pleased that Exfoliant had become so eco-friendly. Plastic synths were notoriously difficult to suppress.

"Can I keep their guns to play with?" asked Alice.

"No."

"Awww."

"They were a bit early," Deltress observed. "Hardly allowed you time to fix the button."

"They didn't factor in his session with Sister Flagella," Zozara said snidely.

"MIN really does want me dead," said Vooq miserably. "Won't there be other attempts?"

"Yes, but don't worry. If you leave me a DNA sample I'll prepare a 3D construct for them to kill. You do realise you'll have to stay on Earth, don't you? Are you happy with that?"

"I think I could be."

"Excellent. And now, have you decided what to do about your button? The fate of Bellicosia rests with you."

"Well," Vooq said slowly, "it's all about equality, isn't it? Bringing both sides into line. If I create a quantum interface implosion, Exfoliant will have a defence network they can't use. If they try, their own suns will destabilise."

"But surely they'll just reverse what you've done?"

"Not possible, due to the observer effect. They'll spring the trap themselves when they inspect my work, and the change isn't time-reversible. Now, could I have some table space please? *All* the table? I'm calling down the portable lab."

The two women gave him room to set it up. Deltress made tea. When his task was complete, Alice brought him ice cream.

"Friends?" he inquired.

"Friends."

"How will we earn a living?" asked Zozara, ever practical.

"I'll be an inventor, I suppose," said Vooq. "I should be able to give this planet some things it needs. Hyperdrive, anyone?"

Pursuit
(Marise Morland)

A state of war had existed between the Reyrith and the Dremm before recorded history began. The two species had spread across half the galaxy, with ceaselessly patrolled borders and fiercely contested territories. The days of sending living beings to fight had long passed, succeeded by automated war machines. These grew in sophistication until all vessels, and the bases which supported them, were equipped with self-determination and no concept of surrender. And thus, after every inhabited world was pulverised and dead, the conflict continued.

Reyrithian battlescout 12-20 was a veteran of combat. It had been constructed in the early days of full automation and had only first-generation AI. Its speed and precision under fire, plus an element of sheer luck, had sustained it. But now it was in urgent need of an overhaul and reboot. Its for'ard heat shield was defective, its outer hull was scarred and pitted by enemy fire, and the bulkheads protecting its sensory array were weakening. It had many times checked itself into orbiting maintenance units, only to leave unserviced by the depleted equipment. Each time, it had notified Command of the problem. Command had not responded.

12-20's mission was to seek, pursue and destroy Dremm ships. It had no other purpose. It followed a random course, as Dremm battle computers would have detected any pattern. The part of the galaxy in which it now found itself was designated neutral, which meant that either side could be maintaining a presence there. And true to expectations, after only seven Reyrith years it encountered another spacecraft. Scans revealed it to be Dremm in construction, though overlarge for combat; and although it had defensive shields, 12-20 could detect no weaponry. Obviously it had malfunctioned, leaving the Dremm ship with one option: flight. It acted accordingly.

12-20 gave chase. Its target's Drive systems were in optimum condition, but its size meant that ultimately it could not outrun the ancient Reyrith scout. 12-20 calculated that the Dremm would be in range of its weapons in two years.

As was its custom when engaged in a lengthy chase, it engaged what was left of its self-repair systems and attempted to improve its performance. It was evaluating these attempts when an interruption came, and its reaction was as close to irritation as its mental capacity allowed.

The Dremm ship was trying to communicate. Its first three efforts didn't match any of 12-20's stored language profiles, but it understood most of the fourth. The message, in dispassionate machine-code, read: Let us go. We are unarmed. We are the last of the Dremm, seeking a new home in another galaxy.

12-20 consulted its database, and finding nothing which forbade communication with the enemy, informed the Dremm that taking all factors into account, such a mission would fail.

There is always hope, came the reply, and belatedly 12-20 realised that the message had been a distraction. The Dremm fugitive was headed for the corona of a star, intending to skirt the outer edges in the belief that its shields would save it. 12-20 was unlikely to survive such a manoeuvre. But it was almost within weapons range, and its course did not deviate. Both craft hurtled toward the unknown sun.

Finally, damaged almost to extinction, the Reyrith emerged from the searing heat and, with what remained of its sensors, scanned for its adversary. There was nothing. It could have escaped harm, or burnt up, or simply be eluding detection. The truth was irrelevant. The chase was over.

The AI which was 12-20 still had a few moments of awareness. It prepared a last report for Command. The data was corrupted but the dying scout sent it anyway, including the exchange with the Dremm. Its hypergate relay was defunct, leaving only the radio spectrum for transmissions.

At the speed of light, 12-20's last databurst travelled the war-torn galaxy, past derelict solar systems, disinterested nebulae and an abundance of gas clouds where new stars were forming. Only one fragment remained of the ruined data, one message for the unknowable future:

There is always hope. There is always hope.

I'm in Charge
(Marise Morland)

The insult could neither be borne nor dismissed. In one swift movement the Comte removed his glove and slapped his rival's face with it. "Name your seconds, m'sieur. Have them wait on mine!"

A few days later, in a country park at dawn, the duellists stood back to back, pistols raised. They each took ten paces, turned and fired. One figure fell. Far off, in a waiting coach, a girl screamed.

"Oi! What're you doin' ere? I told you before, you ain't welcome."

"I came to see my boy. I've got a right to see Tarquin."

"No you ain't. Tarquin's not your son."

"You always were a liar, Shaz."

"'E ain't yours. If you want proof, try asking your brother who the father is. Now get out of my pub!"

The Andromedan fleet was assembled along the spiral edge of the Milky Way galaxy. The Thousand World Alliance, equal in strength and numbers, stood ready to retaliate. It was a conflict which would doubtless result in the destruction of many star systems. On board the Andromedan flagship, the mad Empress gave the order to launch the first wave of battle drones.

"Do you ever think that we're all part of a simulation and that someone's having a laugh at our expense?"

"I've seen the film."

"I don't just mean the Earth. I meant everywhere! The whole universe! I was talking to this bloke and he reckons we've got no free will, that there's a secret agenda..."

"Cor. Shaz ain't half giving Neville what for."

"Aren't you listening to me?"

"Yeah, but – this is more entertaining, innit?"

"Grid Operator Pifl, Fourth Class, there seems to be an excess of conflict in your sector. Would you care to explain?"

"My characters are an inquisitive bunch, Team Leader. I think it best to keep them occupied locally."

"Agreed. We don't want another break-out. But this intergalactic war seems a little overblown. Don't waste your resources on it."

"It's a stand-off, not a war. Someone will assassinate the Empress and a truce will be agreed. Lots of celebrations all round, everyone feels good and is content with their lot. Just as the elite desire."

"All hail the elite! Well, carry on, Pifl. But you'd better take out that conspiracy theorist."

"Consider it done."

"What are you doing, Azrael?"

"Oh, sorry, God, I didn't see you there. I was preparing to smite these upstarts, these – elite – for daring to presume they are lords of all they survey. Everyone knows that's *you*."

"Yes, yes, quite. Just refrain from smiting, if you don't mind."

"I'm the Angel of Death. It's what I do."

"Well, we'll have to find another outlet for your talents. Ever thought of joining a heavy metal band?"

"That's more in Lucifer's line, isn't it? Maybe I should pay him a visit."

"And start another feud? Let him alone. Haven't you realised how miserable we've become lately? It's all vengeance and mayhem. Positively apocalyptic. And I've had enough of it. Assemble the Archangels. We're going back to the Age of Noise – a joyful noise. Everyone will be at their luminous best, and I shall put on my most benign, most radiant, most effulgent countenance."

"We're going to be – nice?"

"You've got it. Now get on with it. Tell Gabriel to bring his trumpet. Oh, just one more thing."

"Yes, God?"

"How do you spell effulgent?"

"Excellent work," remarked the Greater One to the entity which, in the far future, would become the next Greater One. "You have chosen the flattened disc shape for each of your universes and stacked them vertically to make optimum use of your space-time allocation. I note that you have disallowed contact between each universe, but permitted interaction at lower levels. Is this set to continue?"

"For now," the Lesser One replied. "It is intriguing, is it not, to see these elites under the illusion that they are in control. If at any time their arrogance no longer engages me, I shall issue a correction."

"And you believe your immersive games will be useful to our fledglings?"

"I do. The categories are Duellists, Soap Opera, Space Invasion and Elite at Work. Our junior administrators need to understand the vicissitudes of organic life."

"And what of Heaven? This is your oldest creation. Does it still serve a purpose?"

The Lesser One gave the equivalent of a sigh. "Possibly not. But it still has the capacity to surprise."

"I can almost feel sorry for your God," admitted the Greater One. "He's very self-possessed, for an illusion. Well, keep up the good work. I'll be back in an aeon for your next appraisal."

"Greater One, may I ask one question?"

"That depends on what it is."

The Lesser One paused indecisively. "This may impact on my future status, but – how *do* you spell effulgent?"

Sustenance
(Marise Morland)

Teon, apprentice Weavewright, was receiving his first assignment. The Weave which underpinned the cosmos was under increasing strain as the universe expanded. And always, the elements of chaos and uncertainty sought to undermine the Weavewrights' patient efforts to maintain it.

Intelligent life, and the worlds which harboured it, could, if nurtured, assist the Weave and save its protectors aeons of work. Certain beings on these worlds, carefully selected by the Weave archivists, produced beautiful art through which the Weave observed itself and knew itself to be strong.

"And just occasionally," the Weavemaster concluded, "we find a new recruit on these worlds."

"An undiscovered Weavewright?"

"Yes. But you're not likely to find one – not on your first foray into strange territory. Here is a shortlist of three artists we believe to be capable of local weavework. Their world needs their input. Good luck."

***

Henri de Toulouse-Lautrec glared suspiciously at Teon. "Did my mother send you?"

"No. Why should she?"

"It wouldn't be the first time she's had her lackeys scour the brothels in search of me. Well, that was a very pretty speech you made, but you can tell your employer that great universal themes don't interest me. I'd rather paint these women. Look at them, *les cocottes*. Splendid, aren't they? So, unless you want to avail yourself of their services, I suggest you leave before Gustave over there throws you out." He leant back in his chair and tipped the brim of his hat over his eyes. Teon saw Gustave advancing and made his escape.

Vincent van Gogh was equally hostile. "Are you here to make trouble or just to make fun? Don't bother with excuses. Why else would you approach me with a story like that? I'm not famous, I've nothing to show you. No, I don't paint flowers, but maybe that isn't such a bad idea. They wouldn't keep talking at me and telling lies. Why are you still here?"

Teon tried an apology and retreated. This wasn't going well. His adopted persona was flawless – the archivists never made continuity mistakes – so he was beginning to think his approach was in question. His third and final contact seemed doomed before he'd said a word. He was standing next to an abandoned building, one of several, and a young man in jeans and hoodie was busy stencilling street art on a relatively smooth piece of wall.

Teon coughed politely. "Excuse me. Are you the artist known as Banksy?"

He turned and grinned. "Aww. Busted! No, seriously, I'm not him. But sometimes people mistake my work for his, just as you did."

So the archivists are not *infallible.* Teon studied the picture more closely. In the foreground, all the detritus of a city street – litter, a cardboard shelter, a homeless man. And further off, a young girl gazing steadfastly at a full moon. "Does this piece have a title?"

"No. Not much point in naming it. Someone'll be here tomorrow with a wrecking ball."

"That's a shame. This work should be seen."

"Oh, it will be." The young man scrolled rapidly through images on his phone, then photographed the mural. "I'm Zack, by the way. Twenty-seven more likes since we've been talking!"

"This may seem a little redundant," said Teon, and delivered his usual speech.

"I get that. It's beautiful."

Teon hesitated. This human seemed so self-assured. Could he possibly be a latent Weavewright? Or was this some kind of a test? "If you want to know more, be at the vanishing point at sunrise tomorrow," he said obscurely. It was a risk. If Zack asked how such a thing was possible, the Weavemaster would disqualify Teon there and then.

But Zack merely smiled. "Will do."

At first light, he returned with some carefully chosen spray paints and markers. On an east-facing part of the wall he created a level landscape basking in sunlight. On its horizon he lovingly blended land and sky in shades of green and gold.

The first rays of the real sun touched the mural. It seemed to shimmer once. Zack had disappeared. Presently the demolition gang arrived, and shortly afterward Teon's portal was safely reduced to rubble.

The invigorated Weave settled down to contemplate itself.

Roxette
(Marise Morland)

<u>Katie</u>

He's late. He won't let me down tonight, surely? He won't let Roxette screw things up.

I make all the usual preparations to welcome him home. I order dinner, put on a dress he likes to see me in, and lay the table for two. Then I gaze out of the apartment window at the cityscape, and see the landing flare of a long-haul shuttle heading for the spaceport. I'm so certain he's on that flight. And when I realise he isn't, I start on the wine.

Soon, I tell myself, he'll come noisily in, with all the gear I wish he'd leave behind just once. I've convinced myself that the day he arrives emptyhanded, he'll have finished with Roxette. But he always brings it – a reminder of his other life, a mute statement that he'll be going back. I wonder if I should tell him to stay away. But instead, I just have more wine. Roxette has won, this time.

<u>Adam</u>

I don't know when this message will arrive, Katie, as the outgoing server's backed up. I expect you've been trying to call me too, after I didn't show up for our anniversary. I don't expect instant forgiveness but please accept that if there had been any way to avoid this delay I'd have been there with you. I don't need to remind you that Roxette was part of my life before I met you, and you said you could handle it. Do you really think it would be any better if I were with you twenty-four seven? We'd drive one another crazy, or even worse, get bored. But since we know our time together is finite, why can't we try to cherish it and each other? Goodbye, my amazing little wife. I'll be home before you know it.

Mandy
He said what? How patronising is that? And how many cancellations does this make? I don't know how you put up with it, I really don't. If he was mine I'd kick him out. Seriously, I think you need to look at the bigger picture. You're trying to deal with this all alone, apart from me that is, and there's no need to. What do I mean? Well, Adam's not the only man to be involved with Roxette, is he? There have always been others, probably with wives. Find them, start a support group. And if that isn't your thing, I can always fix you up with an intro or two. Live a little, that's all I'm saying. I've gotta go – my date will be here in a minute. See you!

Waylon
Mrs. Treadaway, this is Waylon Harkness, captain of the mining scow Roxette. I'm afraid I have some bad news about your husband. The Roxette was being refuelled for its next trip to the asteroid belt when some space debris holed its propellant and pressurised gas tanks. The escaping fuel started a fire. Adam boarded the scow, uncoupled it from the Orbiter and singlehandedly guided it to a safe distance before the explosion which destroyed it. His brave sacrifice saved all our

lives. With your permission I'll return his personal effects as soon as I'm earthside. My condolences, ma'am.

Mandy's vlog

So, followers, we have more breaking news about widow Katie Treadaway and her beau of just one week, Waylon Harkness. Pending an inquiry, hunky astronaut Waylon has been reassigned to ground duties at only a third of his former salary. And Katie is facing eviction as apparently the constantly distracted Adam omitted to pay the bills. Does the curse of Roxette live on? You bet it does. Roxette 2 is on the launch pad as I speak. So lock up your husbands, astro-girls. She's out there!

Crowning Achievement
(Marise Morland)

Greetings one and all! At last the time has arrived, and we welcome all civilisations between here and the Galactic Rim to the semi-final of the nine hundred and ninety-ninth ESP-fod. Very shortly we'll go live to the planet Evanescent, where twin stadia have been set up for two of the remaining entrants. The winner will then compete against the third semi-finalist. The contest, as many of you will know, requires the competitors to re-enact a famous event from their world's history. A million esper-drones are in geostationary orbit above Evanescent, ready to convey every unforgettable moment to you, our wonderful audience. Those of you who are not telepathic will find our immersive quantumcast almost as fulfilling. Our semi-finalists are the Crown Protectorate of Brexit, representing their homeworld Sol Three, who will interpret the Coronation of Queen Elizabeth the Second; and the Empire of Umbroloozia, who will recreate their victory over the marauding Zebulons. The Crown Protectorate will perform first. We now hand control to the presentation crew. Let the ESP-fod begin!

"Cue rain."

"Copy."

"Cue hologram of Westminster Abbey."

"Cue choirboys. I said, cue choirboys."

"Sorry Marcus. Crispin's been sick."

"Send in the cleaning bots."

"No time!"

"Then sling a flag over it. Cue full choir. Cue heralds."

They watched. Half a galaxy watched.

"The procession looks the part," Shireen ventured.

"It does," Marcus agreed. "If we can pull this off we'll be lauded back home."

"Loaded," Shireen corrected.

"That too. Cue Archbishop."

The Archbishop spoke in mellifluous tones.

"He's making it up as he goes along," muttered Shireen.

"Relax. This lot won't know the difference. Now for my latest embellishment."

"Marcus! What have you done now?"

"Watch."

The Archbishop lowered the bulky, ostentatious crown onto the Queen's dainty head. Except that it remained poised, just touching her hair. She rose to leave the Abbey. The crown stayed with her.

Shireen glared,

"It was so heavy," Marcus said by way of an excuse. "Evanescent's gravity's stronger than ours. It's just a little stasis field. The impeller's in her collar."

"We didn't have stasis fields in 1953," Shireen pointed out.

"So what? This is art!"

Eight thousand worlds voted their approval.

"See? Now shut up. Cue more rain, cue the Mall. Cue coach."

The coach wasn't gold, of course. The budget didn't allow for that. It was nickel electroplated steel. Holographic crowds, a few real people to the fore, waved and cheered.

"I've had to truncate the mileage, of course," Marcus continued with growing confidence. "Just initialising the Palace gates now…"

The coach shed a wheel. Marcus swore. The other participants, mostly soldier-actors, helped the occupants dismount and escorted them through the gates with commendable dignity. The presentation ended, leaving the coach lying drunkenly on one axle.

"Well, we tried," Marcus said resignedly. "Come on. We're done here."

Meanwhile, in the adjoining stadium, the battle between the Umbroloozians and the Zebulons was under way. A hovering weapons platform with a faulty gyro suddenly lost position, its particle beam striking the abandoned coach.

If the coach had been real gold, as the publicity had stated, it would have melted but absorbed the blast. The electroplating, however, reflected the energy back at its source. The beam projector exploded with an incandescent bang, followed by the rest of the linked array. When the rubble settled, there was nothing left of Stadium Two but a crater.

"The Crown Protectorate is through to the final by default," announced the ever-enthusiastic AI. "They will compete against the Stompscar Federation, three times winner of the ESP-fod. Its latest entry will be the suppression of the black hole which once threatened the planet."

"Why does it have to be *them*," groaned Marcus. "We might as well go home now."

"No, let's get pissed and *then* go home," Shireen said.

They were awakened by the remorseless AI making an announcement. "Breaking news! We have just learned that Stompscar's entire solar system has vanished. Obviously a serious mishap in rehearsals! We therefore declare the Crown Protectorate of Brexit the winner."

"Well, isn't that nice," said Marcus hazily. "Goodnight."

"Haven't you forgotten one little detail?" asked Shireen.

"Forgotten…?"

"We're the winners. So we have to do the whole thing over again, starting now. Well, say something!"

"Cue the rain?"

Caballo Chronicles:
The Nocturnals vs. The Boondockers
(Chris Rodriguez)

As Christine Rasmusdottr uttered the memory that chronicled their previous meeting, the words turned to ash and fell onto the pages of The Time Keeper in runic form. Once spoken, the tales of The Nocturnals would live only in the realm of the dead. The new word, "Boondockers" was included in this entry. The Time Keeper was retrieved periodically by The Originators so records were required daily.

The Nocturnals feared The Boondockers, the sun worshippers, with their bows and arrows made from Hawthorne. If their hearts were pierced by these deadly weapons, the Nocturnals would become as ash like the words. Since the Boondockers had suspected an alien-type presence in their midst at the beginning of this snowbird season, The Nocturnals congregated and hunted only while the others slept. The Nocturnals were used to this kind of life. The Boondockers were not their only enemy. Not by a long shot. Once the entries were made, they continued their meeting in the circle.

"Is that a new wrap? How did you get that lovely red thread in there?" Christine asked Diane.

"Yes, the moon is waxing and my skin is becoming dry and burnt. I needed the extra cover." Diane Van Helsing (no relation to the Dutch vampire Hunter) sported the rosy hued porcelain skin of her ancestors. It was as delicate as silk. "The red is nice, isn't it? A small thread of life. It came from the heads of a mother and daughter Miles ensnared in our traps. I understand it's a rare color among these people, the migrant hordes from the south."

Miles, Diane's husband, nodded in agreement, his long blonde locks wound and unwound continuously like mating snakes. "She weaves a strong net for the traps as well." His eyes flashed green in approval.

Diane smiled in return. Their spirits, like the spirits of all Night people floated about them like mist, forever attached like the shadows of living folk, seemingly stitched to their feet, but could never be brought inside. Tendrils from each ran across the space between them and tentatively touched before retreating.

Jon Scott Vjeski glided across the open path to join the group, his hounds pulling at their restraints. Ectoplasmic ropes ran from all the members to touch the majestic heads of the animals, to pay homage to their importance in this new life. He nodded in greeting to the others and quietly sat. His silver hair crowned his head in spikes and eyes the color of polished copper dropped to the ground. He listened quietly and respectfully to the speakers.

Gregor Stijn, already seated, laid one hand upon his small bitch to quiet any intention of her joining the hounds. Platinum clouds of hair swirled like cumulus climbing aloft and rolling down, then piling high again. His eyes, icy blue like the glaciers of his Norwegian homeland kept watch. He swirled the frozen cubes in his tumbler then sipped. "Mmm.

This is a particularly good drink you mixed tonight, Mary," His spirit mostly kept to itself lapping quietly around his feet, ebbing and flowing gently like the movement of the cold northern lakes. Everyone grunted in agreement.

"It's spicy! What did you add to it?" Diane asked.

Maryanne Tsis tsis 'tas, medicine woman and wife of Aaron, shook out her raven hair braided with turquoise and sinew. "I think it must have been from the Mexicans. The chilis they eat, you know?"

Jon's hounds had flushed out some illegals hiding in the wash the night before. "You should come with us, Christine," he commented. "It's been a long time since you hunted."

"Oh, it's too far even with my walking sticks," commented the eldest of the group and first to be placed in this RV Ranch in Tucson. "And I can no longer fly. I'd just slow you down." She took a sip of her drink and also remembered to thank Mary for the meal.

Aaron, black-haired like his wife but with threads of gray shot through his chest-length beard, stood across the circle from his mate. He glowed with pride and their young spirits ran swiftly to the center to embrace. The tendrils twined and slow-danced together for a moment before retreating to the heels of their bodies. "Mary makes the best Bloody Mary's. The perfect blend of alcohol spirits, blessings and life essence!" As a Cheyenne shaman, Aaron understood the importance of prayer, ceremony, song, and dance if called for. He often participated in the healings.

"And made all the better with Gregor's new ice machine," Christine noted as she lifted her cup to toast everyone present. Her dry, silver hair flew away from her face, then settled again, her movements restricted by age.

Miles cleared his throat for attention and when the murmurs of appreciation died down, he recounted his clandestine presence at the meeting of The Boondockers last evening. He reported a group of rockhounds were planning a dig for crystals at a local mine. Caballo Loco RV Ranch was famous for the numerous mines and generous pockets of gemstones in the area. The coyotes and smugglers who brought their own prey across the border 30 miles to the south of the Sierrita Mountains knew the mines well. They were good places to hide from the Border Patrol technology and officers regularly patrolling the area.

Maryanne exclaimed that she would love some new crystals for her collection to use as healing media. Sometimes the essence of their prey made The Nocturnals ill.

"Me as well," Diane chimed in. I would love to weave them into my black-hair cloak so they shine like stars in a night sky."

"We will make a plan then to have Kim join them and gather some materials for us," Christine offered. Kim was the human liaison between The Nocturnals and The Boondockers. Kim also warned the night people whenever The Boondockers celebrated with bonfires and wizardry particularly during hunting season. Those were particularly dangerous times for The Nocturnals to be hunting their prey too close to camp.

The sky was beginning to lighten in the east. Pink waves of cloud flowed over the high craggy peaks across the valley. Jon stood and nodded to the others. "Come hounds. We must rest so we can hunt tomorrow night. Back to our bed of dust!" he commented ruefully. He often let it be known how he missed the cool, fluffy loam of his homeland as he often recollected his sweet-smelling blanket of fir needles before he was transferred to Caballo. The Nocturnals waved a salute as he left the circle.

"We must all go inside soon," Christine warned. "I just want to say how glad I am Mary has returned to the circle. I awoke in terror before dawn this morning when a blinding light filled my camper. I thought it was "them" coming back to take me. I don't know why. It's been decades and there are no more orifices in my body left un-probed."

Gregor chuckled at her description then squirmed, perhaps at his own memories of the abductions they had all endured.

"It was just me coming home from my graveyard shift," Mary sighed. "One of us has to work." Aaron and Mary were the youngest of the group and last to join them at the ranch. Mary was a nurse by trade. Handy during rare times of starvation. "I hope The Originators never return! I loved my normal life before they came."

Christine stood slowly, testing her balance. "We will survive in spite of them. Perhaps we were brought here to thin the hordes from the south so

138

they can re-colonize. Nevertheless, The Star People made us what we are, so now - let us *be* vampires!"

Chico on the Floor
(Rickey Rivers Jr)

1.

We were assigned to different rooms. There were only twelve in my room. In front of us a computer and keyboard. We were instructed to bang sets of buttons like we knew how. Some of us tried learning. Others were frustrated, and then there was Chico.

***

I remember the before times too, when we were free. We had our homes, our simple lives, but all of that was stripped away. The helicopters overhead were first. Then there were drones to survey. Next were footsteps, heavy but quiet. In retrospect it happened so fast.

In the now times I carefully type, as we were instructed. The bright lights of the computer screen means nothing to my now damaged eyes under the artificial room light. My colleagues have nearly given up. I can't blame them. It's been tough.

Our families were segmented. I'm not sure where and in what rooms my brothers lie, but I'm sure they're close. Sometimes I can almost hear them. Sometimes I think I hear many things, like a small chatter, a whisper, from a faraway place. I know this means nothing in the grand scheme, but anything means something when you're locked away from home. A prison, even shaped as such, is still a prison. After all, we're housed in a man-made building, the artificial lights make the rooms seem almost friendly, many small conference rooms, all in a row, the screens line up with the eyes, our eyes all tired from screen staring. I wither. All of us wither away each day, defecation to the sides of us, none of it unusual. All the bright white lights beam down.

I get carried away in confusion when recollecting the thoughts of a better time. I remember when all of this was new, before we were taken to this place. Mostly, I remember Chico.

Chico was made an example of. I remember him making us laugh from time to time, because he, like all of us, had grown tired of the routine. But Chico was rebellious in nature. He threw something at one of our capturers. He refused to work. But this only went on for a day. Soon after, from a small door on the side of the room, came then a man with a black rod in one hand. From this rod was a terrible noise, a vibration. This rod was electrified.

Chico was struck. Chico was beaten and shocked, and we all had to watch, but not watch, and keep our eyes on the screens in front of us. Soon, Chico was dead. I remember the smoke rising up from his body. I remember it reaching the ceiling. I remember the smell of flesh and hair. Chico's eyes weren't eyes anymore. They were simply lumps of pus.

***

Feeding time is reprieve. We at least get that. I don't know why, but the moments of eating, something taken for granted, seem like the most peaceful parts of the day. Though our legs dangle and are shackled to the floor, our hands are free to feed. They must be free to type, albeit restrictively due to shackles around the wrists. But we feed for reprieve, and we work with these same hands, shoveling food into waiting mouths. Our hands, such powerful things; why don't we use them, why can't we, as we have before?

I remember having this thought, this singular thought and with that thought I was alone, but I was only alone for maybe an hour. Soon, I was joined. From a distance, I remember another voice, smaller than I, but a voice all the same. This voice said to me "Enough." Then, once hearing that voice, I heard another. This one said "Risky" These two voices seemed to come from different parts of the building. I knew them. My brethren were talking, but they weren't using sound.

***

Over time I've come to understand this new way of communication. I'm now able to talk to others through simply conjuring the words from a thought. Others respond in kind. One informed me of the black rod used in another part of the building. It wasn't used to kill. It was used to tame. This black rod was only used once. Then, the offender got back to work.

I spoke of Chico to the others. I told them the terrible things I saw, the sounds, the horrible smell of his corpse. They responded with remorse. Then, one voice simply said, "I saw." Without thinking I turned my head away from the computer screen, quickly then hearing "No!" before turning my head back to the screen.

"Keep working," said the voice. "Don't look suspicious."

This voice was one of ours. I did as told. I kept my eyes on the work, all of it babble and nonsense.

2.

Since first recognizing speech was possible through mind transfer I've spoken with several overs over the past few days. I've been informed of the following: this building is several floors high, there are several black rods used to shock and maim, and the guards of the building rotate. We've formulated a plan. This will take place one week from today. On that day we'll be free again.

***

Oh, I dream so sensually about the times of then, the past so far away. I used to be happy in my home. I had a real life then. There was no work, only was there peace. And peace to me is freedom, freedom to exist and not only exist, but to exist without the presence of outsiders and onlookers, gawkers of my kind.

I've heard stories before of others being taken away from homes and sent to places which only house behind bars. A prison is a prison. They've put different names on every sort of prison just to make them seem nicer. But even your own home can be a prison if you don't desire peace.

Peace is a necessity, and I can't have that in these rooms, in this building. None of us have slept well since our capture. And yes, we're allowed sleep, but only for so long. It's never enough sleep to truly run away. In my head I see myself run. It's been so long. Home is too far away.

***

It's almost time. Since lunch is all at once for one floor at a time we'll synchronize. The floor below is first, then us, then the ones above us. I'm not sure how many floors are here, but one group seems not to hear sounds above. By my numbers I'll guess the number eight. There must be eight floors. Depending on the layout of the building we'll go up or down. Down might have guards.

Now, for the signal, it should be heard after lunch. One below will induce vomiting. That will either bring a beating or cleaning. We've planned for both. Grabbing the rod is risky, but grabbing it and the guard at the same time should cause the sort of reaction we're counting on. It's a sacrifice of one for the sake of the whole. We've agreed upon a martyr.

***

The sounds of home call. They voice concern. It's time. Lunch has been delivered below. And now we wait and type and wait some more. It's only a matter of time before our wanted freedom. At least the ones below will be fed. As for the rest of us, we're sure to find food elsewhere. Anywhere but here has to be kind.

"It's happening," I hear a voice.

There's a scream from below. This same scream reminds me of Chico. It scares me. It's hard to describe. It's like a vibrating screech, the torment reverberated, this time twice. There's two in pain. There's commotion, then silence, then nothing.

We type on. Time goes on, and it's slow. I wait for confirmation, but it's so quiet. Only the sounds of typing surround me. My gaze goes from the computer to the walls to the floor to the ceiling. I wonder if others are thinking what I'm thinking. I wonder if they too feel dejection. I wonder this, with almost tears.

Then, loud in my head, I hear "It worked!"

I hear multiple screams below, chaos, wonderful, sweet chaos.

"Kill them all!" I hear.

I hear running, many feet coming from below. Then a door slides open and I'm greeted by my brothers from below. They're salivating, they're covered in blood. Into the room they scramble, all releasing one colleague at a time.

"More guards coming!" I hear.

"Kill them all!"

I'm released. I'm finally free.

"Kill them all!" a voice inside, then another, and another. And I hear the guards coming, but we're united. And I, being with sound mind and body, am fully committed to standing my ground against our capturers.

We'll fight, and we'll fight, and we'll fight some more. We'll fight for us. We'll fight for Chico! We'll fight for all the fallen and locked away. We're united now. This fight is for the apes!

Poster Girl
(Liam A Spinage)

"Silent Night..."

Faith slipped out of the church as the choir began singing another carol and quietly closed the door behind her so as not to disturb them in their moment. Packed inside was most of the town of Salvation, Montana, praying for her best friend, Joy. The vigils had been Faith's idea from the start, bringing the community together in this time of profound loss. Rather than celebrating the miracle of the birth of Christ, they were huddled together inside praying for the safe return of one of their own. Nobody had seen Joy in nearly a month. Nobody knew where or why she had gone. There were no leads, no clues, no ransom demands. Search parties returned each day just before dusk, the hills and the woods being too dangerous to search at night. They had found nothing. So, each night, the town of Salvation did what they did best. They prayed.

"Holy Night..."

It was Christmas Eve, so Faith wanted to believe in miracles now more than any other time. She wanted to believe she'd see her friend again tomorrow, safe and well with a story to tell. Instead, the single candle she held in her gloved hands sputtered in the winter wind as snow flurries blew in continuous circles in the car park around her. Catching a moment of silence outside, she looked up at the heavens and, as she wiped a solitary half-frozen tear from her eye, offered a sincere, solitary prayer.

"All is calm..."

A thin layer of snow peppered the car park, but the clouds above were thick with the stuff. A fresh layer, deep and crisp and even, would put paid to any hope of the search parties, covering any prints, and removing any traces of her friend that might remain. Faith shivered in the chill of the night, but the cold was invigorating, strengthening, somehow, compared with the stifling heat of the crowd. Faith needed a moment alone with God, a pause from the frantic mayhem of the past weeks and the constant attention of the townsfolk's perpetual, penetrating gaze.

"All is bright..."

As she was about to turn and rejoin the vigil inside, something in the hills above the town attracted Virginia's attention. A procession of lights - bright as stars but lower in the sky - began to dance across the horizon, ducking below the silhouetted tree lines on the ridges of the two mountains and then resurfacing. Silvery motes arcing across her vision, beckoning her forth, promising her all would be well. She took three steps gingerly forward, convinced her prayer had been answered but still unwilling to leave her father the Rev. Shepherd to manage the congregation alone.

She hesitated for what seemed like a heartbeat but felt like a lifetime. The modern world being what it is, it would later be simple enough to time that pause properly and ascertain that it lasted precisely nine minutes according to the CCTV footage of the church entrance. At the end of that pause for thought, one light in particular shone very briefly and very brightly and Virginia took one more step forward toward the source, raptured by the beauty of that strange glow.

It was to be her final step. Nobody in Salvation ever saw her again. The wind picked up around the chapel, carrying with it flurries of snow that hid her precious last movements and blew an old poster, torn at one edge, onto the church door where it stuck almost in defiance. The poster read: Missing. Joy Carpenter, aged 15. Please contact Sheriff Carpenter in Salvation with any details. Between these sentences was nestled a slightly grainy black and white photo of a young girl, smiling through pearly white teeth, a pair of glasses jammed into a bun of dark hair rather than resting on her nose.

Nobody noticed Faith was missing at first. Not like Joy, whose absence had been picked up and reported almost immediately. There was a singular advantage, after all, in being the daughter of the sheriff, even if that relationship was somewhat strained by the natural problems of bringing her up as a single parent with a busy job, not to mention the nascent rebelliousness of teenage years. The community had brought the three girls up: Joy, Faith and their friend Hope, all daughters of prominent townsfolk. They raised them with good Christian values and a respect for their family and community which would have been the envy of other parents, had Salvation ever had visitors from outside except for the odd hunter or hiker. The three had been inseparable, the loss of Joy had left the others inconsolable.

Without Joy, though, the cracks had started to appear in their otherwise picture-perfect community. While nobody could conceive of a bad word to say against any of the girls, there were others upon whom scrutiny and suspicion fell in equal measure. Accusations of impiety began as mere whispers then rose in volume and frequency with each passing day Joy remained undiscovered.

Sheriff Carpenter, distraught and sleepless at the loss of his only daughter, called a town meeting at which he could barely contain his grief and others, particularly those with youngsters themselves, could barely contain their fear and anger. The Reverend Shepherd urged calm: for the first time in his career, he realized that his loyal congregation weren't listening to him.

"Keep faith," he repeated ad nauseam, "The Lord moves in mysterious ways. Keep faith and we will find Joy again." This offered less comfort than he imagined: he was terrified himself, incensed that something so horrific should happen to Salvation, to the little town where, like so many others around him, he had been born and lived his entire life.

Meanwhile, the lives of the three girls were laid bare. They were constant companions, had no romantic interests they were willing to divulge, had lived blameless, selfless lives helping to cook and deliver food for the elderly. None of them had been in the slightest bit of trouble except for the occasional familial arguments which were always followed by loving reconciliation.

If there was nothing wrong with the town of Salvation, as its population passionately believed, there must be an outside influence. The hotel guest book was scrutinized, every visitor traced and contacted. It all came to nothing.

Missing posters were printed and distributed to other local towns. Unthinkable as it was that Joy might have met her end, it also seemed unthinkable that she might have run away, especially without leaving a note and certainly not without telling her firmest friends. Nothing came of it. It seemed Joy had simply vanished.

Now the same thing had happened to Faith, on Christmas Eve no less. As the vigil continued throughout the night, nobody else left the church until the clear evening had become the dull gray sky of a snowy Montana dawn. When the caroling and prayers ended, the Reverend Shepherd looked frantically for his daughter to help fill the urns of tea and coffee and offer blankets to those who were shivering. When he couldn't find her, he began to call her name over and over, the congregation gradually hushing as their leader became more fraught in his plaintive cries. Sheriff Carpenter went to his side and began to ask the questions that nobody wanted to hear again, questions they could not answer even though in their hearts they all believed somebody must know.

"Is anybody else missing? Who isn't here? When did anyone last see her? Luke, take three others and make an immediate search of the area. Don't worry Reverend, we'll find her. We'll find her."

Thus, the disappearance of Joy ceased to be an isolated incident. If the town was afraid before, it was now in full blown panic, even as they retreated to their own residence to celebrate Christmas. Curfews were imposed in every household. The movements of anyone outside in the snow were scrutinized behind twitching curtains: the switchboard at the Sheriff's office was overwhelmed.

Sheriff Carpenter himself, a stern but fair man with great bearlike arms, listened attentively to young Luke as the search party returned.

"There's no sign of her, Sir. No sign at all. There are only a few footsteps in the snow, just off the porch, and then they vanish into the drift. But there's something up there, you'd best come and see yourself before it gets too blustery."

Following his deputy outside, the Sheriff was certain of two things. Call it a gut instinct underlined with years of police work. Firstly, whatever had happened, the two girls were together somehow. Whether they'd run away or been abducted was something he wasn't sure of - if it was the former there'd be hell to pay - but he was convinced that the same thing had happened to them both. Two missing girls in a town like Salvation couldn't be a coincidence. Secondly, that meant that either their willowy, preppy friend Hope knew something, or she was in danger herself. He'd get to that once he'd taken a look at what his deputy had found.

It was a perfect circle of burnt grass, seared into the ground at the edge of the car park just beyond where Faith's footsteps finally ended. He'd not seen anything like it in his life and had no idea what might have caused it. Luke was busy taking pictures of the scene, as much for his keen interest in the unusual and bizarre as for a record. Sheriff Carpenter nodded to him and asked him to bring Hope to the church as soon as he'd finished.

Back in the church, he found the Reverend seated at a little table in the kitchen, his hands shaking as they gripped a cracked mug of hot coffee, a blanket over his shoulders placed there by his loving wife who stood quietly behind him. They both looked up as the Sheriff entered and shook his head to indicate their lack of progress.

"Who could do this, Sheriff?" The Reverend was openly weeping now. "What manner of evil creature could have taken away our precious girls?"

Removing his hat to reveal a scant growth of graying red hair, the Sheriff shook his head again.

I must admit, I don't rightly know. We'll find them though, mark my words. We'll find them and make them pay. You have my solemn vow."

They stood there in silence for several minutes until they were interrupted by the face of a young girl, framed with disheveled golden locks, eyes red and puffy with weeping, standing in the kitchen doorway. It was Hope.

"No one is accusing you of anything." Sheriff Carpenter was doing his best to put her at ease, but it was clear that young Hope was terrified out of her wits and that his attempts to mollify her anxiety were only making things worse.

"I haven't done anything!" Near hysterical, she turned to the Reverend. "What's happened to Faith? Please, tell me? Why won't anyone tell me what's going on?"

It was Mrs. Shepherd who answered, her husband's head being firmly buried in his hands.

"She's gone, Hope. Just gone. From right outside the church. Please, if you know something, please let us know." Mrs. Shepherd bit a quivering lip to hide her worry, but her pleading words were spoken with a soothing tone.

"These first few hours are usually crucial." The sheriff interrupted. "Luke is organizing search teams…"

"I want to join in. I want to help find her."

"Hope, we need to keep you with us."

"You don't understand! She was my best friend! Of course I'm going to help! You can't stop me!" A grim defiance arose from Hope's tearstained face. Only after she spoke did Hope begin to comprehend what the Sheriff actually meant. She spoke again, faltering and stuttering this time.

"Is…is something going to happen to me too? What's happening?" That last question came out as a near-wail, the last, desperate call of distress and loss.

Luke shuffled in, a sheaf of papers in his hand. From the excited look on his face, it would appear he had a lead. He cocked his head at the sheriff and then over at Hope. Sheriff Carpenter stood up from the little wooden chair, dragging it back under the table as he nodded to the Shepherds.

"Back in a tick." He closed the door on a room of silent sobbing and fretful finger biting and beckoned his deputy to follow him out of earshot.

"What is it? Have you found something?"

Luke shuffled the papers nervously, almost breathless in his excitement.

"You're not going to believe this, boss. It's aliens."

Sheriff Carpenter sighed and massaged his temples. He could feel a migraine coming on and could do without any of his deputy's dubious theories. In the absence of anything else to go on, though, and out of the need to let Luke's prattle run its course, he waved at him to continue.

"I ran some images of that flattened circle of grass through an image search program on the internet." Luke was eager for acknowledgement, but his revelation was lost on the sheriff, whose knowledge of how tech operated began and ended with the patrol car and the fax machine. Undeterred, he continued. "They're similar to these satellite images of crop circles, there are hundreds of them across the US reported every year."

"And how does that prove it's aliens?" Sheriff Carpenter knew he had to draw this to a conclusion, preferably one that wasn't a long, drawn-out explanation. Thankfully, he didn't believe there was one.

Luke looked perplexed. "There's always aliens where there are crop circles, chief! Everyone knows that. And we know nobody in Salvation could be responsible, right?"

The sheriff knew no such thing, as much as he wanted to believe it.

"How does this help us, Luke? You want me to find their alien spacecraft and issue a search warrant?"

"Reckon it's gotta be lurking around here somewhere. Floating above us. It's probably got a cloaking device so we can't detect it."

"Tell you what, why don't you round up a few people and go looking for signs of it in the hills." Anything to get rid of his annoying deputy before his headache really set in. Besides, that would get his deputy back out searching.

Luke beamed. "Sure thing, chief! We're sure to find something! Maybe some more of these strange signs! He reached down to speak into his radio as he left the church, leaving the sheriff alone again.

Back in the kitchen, the Reverend and Mrs. Shepherd sat across the table from Hope. They all had something to say, but none of them were quite able to articulate it. Hope spoke first.

"They've found something, haven't they? That's why they left."

"Oh, sweetie." Mrs. Shepherd took her hands from her husband's shoulders and leaned across the table to take Hope's hands in hers. "They'll tell us if they find anything." She sounded reassuring, but there was a lingering doubt. What could they have discovered? She shuddered at the thought.

"I can't just sit here and do nothing. I just can't. If I..." She jumped as the door creaked open and the sheriff returned.

"Luke is leading a search party." He leant heavily on the little table, wishing the world would stop spinning long enough for him to think clearly. "Meanwhile, Hope, I think it's best you stay here. I'll let your mother know."

Hope balled her hands into little fists and stood up, her hair flicking back from her freckled face. "I want to help. I can't just sit here. Please." She cast her eyes round all the adults in the room anticipating that one of them might agree, but only met blank stares as they exchanged glances.

"We'll come with you." The reverend's voice echoed unexpectedly in the gloomy air of the tiny church kitchen. He looked over at the others.

"Guess we're all going together then. I'll radio through to Luke, let him know we're about to form a second search team." He fiddled with the dial but met only static. "Maybe it's the weather interfering. I'll go outside and call him. See you there. And wrap up warm, for Heaven's sake, it's freezing out there."

They stood with Luke on the ridge just above the town. The deputy was gesticulating wildly and excitedly about something they couldn't quite make out until he shared his camera with them.

"Look at it with the zoom on. You'll see!"

One by one, they did. They saw it all. Where, on the ground, it had looked like a perfect circle, the scorched ground outside the church looked different from up here. There was a crisscross of smaller lines inside the circle itself, visible now only because of their vantage point and because snow had settled along those lines while leaving the rest of the burnt ground untouched. Even with the low midday sun barely piercing the clouds, the fine mesh of lines was bathed in its light.

"Tell me that's an accident." Luke was jubilant. "Tell me that's man made."

"What are you talking about?" The reverend was cross, and it only now dawned on the sheriff that Luke was about to share his crackpot theories with the most devout people in the town. He winced.

"These are clear signs of an alien visitation! There are hundreds of websites devoted to UFOs, if I take a photo and share it..."

"Enough, Luke." Sheriff Carpenter's look said, 'I'm going to kill you for doing this'. Reverend Shepherd's said, 'I'm going to pray for your immortal soul.' His wife just looked confused as she held her husband's arm tightly.

Hope gasped as she lowered the camera. "I've seen that sign before. Joy painted it on her backpack. It's exactly the same, I swear to God." That last comment was directed at the good reverend, lest he doubt her. "I...I don't know what it means, but I think Joy did. She was really happy with how well it came out and showed us both. When we asked what it was, she just smiled, that kind of beatific, all-consuming, all-knowing smile she had sometimes." She looked over at the sheriff.

157

"I only just remembered that. It didn't seem important before."

All eyes turned to the sheriff now, who shuffled uncomfortably. "Yeah, I remember. I was upset with her for ruining her school bag. That was the last argument we had, just a week before she went missing. She apologized the next morning. God, how could I have missed that?"

It was Reverend Shepherd's turn to speak. "I don't remember seeing anything like that in Faith's room. I'm sure I'd remember." He looked over at his wife who nodded silently in agreement.

"Chief, I'm going to head back and run this through an image search, see what it brings up. Maybe it'll give us an idea of where to look. I can take a look in Faith's things as well if that's OK with the Rev.?"

Mrs. Shepherd walked over and handed Luke the keys. "Anything for my Faith."

"I want to keep looking. There might be more of these. There might be other signs. Stay with me?"

It wasn't the way any of them had planned on spending Christmas afternoon, especially the reverend who was worried for his flock. A missing daughter was more important, though, so the four of them spent chilling hours on the outskirts of Salvation, climbing both the local hills to get better vantage points on high to look out on the town as their world lay in solemn stillness with the strife and woe far below them.

As evening drew in and the gentle snowfall of the day gave way to a clear moonlit night, the weary group began to make their way back to Salvation, exhausted and with nothing to show for their efforts. They were about to turn into the pine forest on the hill beneath them when Hope gasped.

"Look! Look over there!" They each turned to where she was pointing, up in the sky on top of the ridge they had just left. Hovering over them, drawing closer as they stared, came a procession of dancing lights, each burning brighter than a thousand stars, lighting up the whole sky now with their brilliance as they flitted toward them in fits and bursts. A mighty dread seized their troubled minds as the glowing orbs grew in size and began to take on a vaguely human shape.

Hope was the first to react. Convinced these strange beings were responsible for taking her friends, she ran toward the lights in a kind of rapt stupor, begging them to take her too so that she might be reunited with them.

Reverend Shepherd, also believing them responsible, fell to his knees even before the aliens reached the clearing and revealed themselves in their full awful phosphorescent presence. "Bring her back! I need her! We all need her! So, help me God, bring her back!"

Mrs. Shepherd stood stock still, paralyzed with fear, awestruck at what she was witnessing.

Sheriff Carpenter began to run after Hope, to bring her back to safety, when a burst of static came over the radio. He buzzed it and heard Luke's excited voice.

"Hey Chief, this is Luke. I was wrong, so wrong. It's not aliens. That sign, it's the sign of the archangel Gabriel. Do you know what that means?".

The Sheriff knew, but was unable to articulate anything beyond "Oh...my...god."

Before them manifested three beings. Their likeness was broadly humanoid in appearance but atop each of their long, translucent necks there were four heads with twelve eyes apiece, atop torsos that sprouted four sets of slowly beating wings. Each in turn was blinded by their brilliance, except for Hope who wept with joy, tears filling her eyes so that she was shielded from the magnificence of their radiance.

"Be not afraid."

The voice, not meant for human ears, boomed. They were all on their knees now.

"I bring you tidings of Joy."

Thus spake the seraph and forthwith appeared a shining throng. Suddenly a great company of all the heavenly host appeared with them.

Glory shone around. The whole town, the whole valley, possibly the whole world now was aglow with their incandescence, their all-seeing luminosity. By the time the group could see again, the visitation was over. The reverend was insensate, irreconcilable. "Take me! By all that is good, it should have been me!"

"Where is she? Where is she?" That was Mrs. Shepherd, desperately trying to find Hope. Sheriff Carpenter joined her, frantically searching in the undergrowth near the new burnt circle where the angel had appeared.

It was too late.

The Shepherds returned, glorifying and praising God for all the things they had heard and seen, but their hearts were empty. Why had the angels taken those young girls to the rapture but spared them? Were they not good enough for the kingdom of heaven? They preached, but their words were as empty as their hearts. Salvation was never the same again as it was after the time they became bereft of Joy, lost Faith and finally were devoid of Hope.

The Orbe Below
(Geoff Nelder)

Far future.

Beyond the Oort Cloud near Alpha Centauri.

A newly-classified minor planet of diameter 2376 km is in orbit around a dying sun. Drone probes all suffer signal failure and disappear. An asteroid-mining supply ship, *Pebble*, is paid by SpaceWeb to investigate using a human crew.

While *Pebble* was a hardened, asteroid-mining work vessel, its cockpit had cushioned faux fur seats, a warm, peach-coloured décor and large console holo screens. The ship couldn't have portholes with such impact-resistant exterior skin. Real lavender and lemon balm plants added an aromatic atmosphere.

Frank Ibsen, growled through his overgrown green beard. "I don't like this mission. I vote to abort. Dido, set a course back to Delta five two."

The raven-haired, much younger woman, laughed. "You're such a wimp, Frank. I vote to continue our mission and rake in the new hefty bonus. Ship, what do you vote?"

A glitch in the programming made their AI sound like its deep voice was under water.

<I have no choice but to vote to continue unless, Frank, you convince me that you and Pebble are at Level nine danger.>

A grunt answered them as Frank jabbed a knuckle-bitten finger at their pale blue console screen.

"Look at it. We don't know what it is. It might not be an actual planet. So smooth. It's just a giant orb. Why are there no impact craters from asteroids and comets? Anyway, how come Ship has a vote. It's not a person."

<A surface entirely of liquid would not have craters.>

Frank muttered as if that meant he couldn't be heard. "But we don't know it is liquid. None of our remote tests can verify that. If it is liquid it won't be safe water but some undetermined slop. Why don't we know more? Because every probe sent down there malfunctions, maybe swallowed. Hardly a ripple and even those designed to survive liquid metals cut off their transmissions just above the surface. We could be in danger up here right now."

Dido waved her delicate fingers over the screen bringing up multi-coloured holo-displays. "Orb is a good name, we'll call it Orbe with an e as in Hamlet. It is too cold for the kind of molten metals that should disable our probes, and it's not radiating anything harmful on the electromagnetic spectrum. It's why we are here with human eyes and senses. We treat it like a suspicious asteroid that might have gaseous outflows. And Ship has a vote as it is a crew member."

"Ship is no more a crew member than the engines and they don't have a vote. You're not suggesting we go down there instead of the robotic probes? If so, you can use a one-girl boat!"

"Not yet, idiot. And Ship has a personality, and a conscience engines do not. Frank, you've got the checklist. We're to send floating drones to hover just above the surface with continuous transmissions. Isn't this exciting, Frank? We might discover something completely new!"

"Bugger something new if it disappears us."

Dido brought up the specs for the drones and entered the atmospheric pressures and wind velocities they've measured.

"Ship, make the necessary mods to a Mark eight drone and release it."

<Done.>

Frank threw his recycled drinking cup into the holographic display of the planet. "If you need me I'll be in my spacesuit in one of the escape pods. How do you know that Ship has a conscience?" His cup attracted ripples and diffraction moire patterns the colours of the rainbow until the static threw it back out where it parabolically flew to the deck.

Dido smelled the decaff chocolate release and tried to spot the nanobots reclaiming the molecules but those, of course she could only imagine. Even so, after a few seconds no drops were visible, spirited away into recycling.

She watched the probe's heat shield glow as it entered the atmosphere then fall away as it unpeeled like an orange to allow the drone to fly down. A second drone stayed aloft to monitor with a telescope. Dido controlled the drone to hover a hundred metres above the smooth metallic-blue surface. If it was liquid then surely there'd be waves? There was an atmosphere of 96% carbon dioxide and 4% nitrogen, which, along with solar radiation from the nearby sun, must generate winds. Radar and other echo-sounding bounced off the surface with no harmful effects. Just a trace of magnetism detected. She dropped the drone to ten metres above the surface. Now the radiometry became haywire, static was heard on the radio transmission. She ordered it to rise again and erratically, it did. From a kilometre above the surface she dive-bombed it. Surely, it would at least make a dent or scar the surface?

Just before impact all telemetry from it blanked. The magnified image from the watching drone went blurry for a few seconds then cleared. There was no sign of the smashed probe. The surface looked smooth from one kilometre but when magnified it had a slight golf-ball appearance with the dimples less than three centimetres deep.

While *Pebble* was orbiting Orbe, a gravimeter monitored for gravity anomalies.

"Hey, Frank, you're missing the experiments. Gravity is higher than you'd expect for something the size of Pluto. It's nearly nought point nine gee, twelve times higher than an average rock planetoid of that size. It might be packed with dense minerals."

"I'm coming."

Within a minute he was standing next to her. "It could be worth a fortune."

She smiled. "Have you changed your vote about aborting?"

"Hell, yeah."

<I hate to interrupt your celebration but there might not be minerals or anything worth retrieving on Orbe. There might be other causes for the higher-than-expected gravity readings, including instrument error. And I have a conscience.>

Frank grunted. "Don't be such a wet fish. What's next on the checklist?"

Dido tapped the screen. "Organic proximity. We've only subjected Orbe to inorganic probes. I can't see that it would react to organic stuff really. We never bother when sussing out asteroids. Anyway, Ship has a conscience because it can say so. Have you heard the engines mention anything?"

<Testing with organics proximity is on the checklist for unknown objects in space. Orbe is unknown.>

"All right, Ship," Dido said. "Keep your hair on, I wasn't going to skip it. Hey, Frank, you're organic, right?"

He scoffed back. "In the olden days humans used monkeys, rabbits and dogs to experiment on, didn't they? Why didn't we bring some?"

"We've become civilized, Frank. Most of us. Now, we could use you, or these lab-grown blocks of genetically modified jelly. Ship, ready a probe with the organic jelly and launch. I'll program it from here to hover at a hundred metres above sea-level."

<Done.>

Twenty minutes later the drone left its heat shield and flew to 100 metres asl where it zig-zagged over a 10-kilometre square area constantly pinging the surface with sensing transmitters and relaying data back to *Pebble*.

Frank muttered through his beard. "Nothing is happening. I think I'll take a shuttle down and play with the damn Orbe. I heard the engines cough yesterday, so they're crew."

<There is a reaction. A subsurface density wave is following the probe. Not shown visually yet, but look at the infrasound radar-cum-sonar real-time mapping. It indicates what I might call a lump moving.>

Dido laughed. "Yes, look how slow it is when I made the probe go more than walking speed! I'll hover it to let the Orbe lump catch up."

Frank was still mostly in his spacesuit from earlier but was doing it up again when he changed his mind. "Whoa, I'm not going down there. Is that a Loch Ness Monster coming out of the surface?"

Dido increased the magnification while making the probe rise five more metres, then twenty as a lump of what looked like mercury but with black and green speckles rose slowly up as if sniffing the probe.

She tapped her finger on her console to keep elevating the sampler. "It didn't do that with the inorganic probes. Perhaps it's hungry. Yet, it's not in a hurry. Ship makes life decisions for us, engines don't."

Frank shouted at her, "Zap it with a laser, see what happens?"

<It would be prudent to use sensors to examine it rather than provoke—>

"Nah, blast it with something, throw a rock, anything. Show it who's boss!"

Dido shook her black hair sending motes into the holo-display. "Show it who's childish, you mean. Ship is right, this is an opportunity to send microbots into it while it's sticking its neck out, so to speak. Ship, ready another probe to do that."

<Will do but I fear Orbe will not wait.>

"Rubbish," Frank said, "Look it's going back down. Oh."

At that moment a slug of grey stuff shot up out of the neck of the 'monster' and grabbed the probe, which disintegrated in two seconds.

<I have a nasty feeling about this.>

Dido nodded. "Me too. It was as if it had been waiting years for a bit of organic food. Hey, look there are three more necks sticking out of the surface, Now more. Many more!"

"Told you we should've zapped it."

<It is as if it now realises the probes, while inorganic—except that one—have come from organic origins. You two.>

Frank laughed uncomfortably. "They're rising up higher but they're not going to reach us at over three thousand kilometres, surely?"

Dido was the first to notice one of the necks separating from the surface and continuing upwards. "How would it find us? It's created more of those probe-smashing slugs and...I think we should leave."

<SpaceWeb will want to know what it is. I have a theory.>

168

"It's a giant brain, isn't it?" Frank blurted out to a forced laugh from Dido.

<Possibly, but I believe it is an expansive knot of organic nanobots linked by neuron-like connections and energised by what seems to be a fluid.>

Frank laughed. "In other words, a giant brain!"

Dido frowned. "We can't test that hypothesis without a sample. I wonder if a really fast probe like we use to go through solar coronas…"

<I will arrange it. Launching a hardened sample probe in five.>

"Good," Dido said, "Meanwhile run stats on those…nine slugs leaving the surface. See if they're on an intercept course for us, though surely not?"

"Hell fires, they are!" Frank yelled. "Let's get out of here, but they'll not follow us for long. Will they? Look they're so small, only fifty centimetres across."

Dido took *Pebble* out of orbit. "Perhaps it depends on how hungry they are."

Ten minutes later they saw all nine slugs had reached escape velocity and were headed towards them.

<I can still launch high speed probes to punch through one and relay data. Shall I, Dido?>

"Yes, meanwhile where should we go?"

"Turn round and attack. It's the best form of defence."

"Frank, we have no weapons. Our laser beams can push small rocks and cut a small hole but—"

"We have all kinds of explosives we use on asteroids!"

"Okay, we use robots to place those after surveying and making risk assessments. If you do that I'll let you launch a robot with an asteroid-busting explosive at one of them. However, they're gaining on us."

<I believe our explosives would create many more of them. I cannot determine their means of propulsion. Some kind of quantum pinching of the timespace in front of them. In which case unless their energy resources will deplete, they will overtake us in twenty-two minutes and five seconds. I recommend we release mass chaff and use our quasi-fusion drive to reach SpaceWeb's custom wormhole QM4513, the nearest. I doubt the slugs would survive a dive through that.>

"True," Dido said, "We can only do so because of the custom encrypted phase changes aliens wouldn't know about."

***

Dido finished dictating her report, attaching all the relevant data streams. "You were right, Ship, it's been an hour since we emerged from the wormhole and they've not followed."

<I wish I was correct. I think they've just emerged.>

Frank, on his third celebratory mockalk drink yelled, "Hell fire! Does that mean what I think it means?"

"Not that I'm one to remotely consider your thoughts, Frank, but it means we cannot go home, or even head for any SpaceWeb colony or sphere of operations."

170

Frank threw his drink at the wall. "Told you Ship shouldn't have the vote not to abort."

Dido shouted, "Stop doing that, Fraaa—ah. Frank, you're a genius! Ship, use our stores to assemble probes. Arm them with billions of cleaning nanobots. We can use them as a kind of antibacterial antibot. What do you think, Ship?"

<Worth a shot.>

Dido ordered Ship to release a monitoring probe to observe the battle.

Frank bounced on his seat with unsuppressed excitement.

Dido gave up trying to calm him. "Just as well that's a gel lemon tube you have instead of a drinks carton."

"Look, Dido, there's a probes and another. How far to release our cleaning nanobots?"

"Another ten minutes and we'll need to magnify the image. Ah the lead probe has released a cloud."

Frank slurped and said, "The other probes have too. Sock it to them kids!"

After a few minutes the slugs appeared to grow larger.

Dido used the quantum-dynamic engines to full power to accelerate away even though she knew the slugs would merely track and follow. "Damn them!"

Ship's deep, gargling voice came over. "Not so. Our cleaning nano-bots had infiltrated and now the slugs are expanding as they disintegrate. We have had a fortunate escape."

Frank celebrated with a long slurp of his lemon gel. "Saved by cleaners."

Doppler Effect
(Geoff Nelder)

Engineer Ding finally brought his Escape Pod under control. It had been ejected from the Mercury Space Station after an asteroid hit but then ricocheted off other debris. Lucky to be alive. The pod's computer was preprogrammed to land in the narrow just-habitable zone on Mercury between the blisteringly hot sunlit and freezing unlit hemisphere.

A proximity alarm jarred his ears. It was another escape pod heading towards him. They should miss by eleven metres at a combined speed of 442 kmh.

Ding's computer identified the incoming escape pod and opened a radio channel.

EP1 to EP2, Engineer Ding here. I am alone in this escape pod. Identify yourself please? Over.

EP2: Dy3xcdf dllil@ 4soku4s 9"idang s@#she e~43hdp disisii dnDang dielswl beb$5" aav5k%c dlvk>g weiie4) lFkrfd

EP1: Ding to EP2 you're coming over as gobbledygook my astronaut friend. If you are decoding this sensibly please start and end with your id and Over. Ding. Over.

EP2: Da&m57 ,,,ddt ie_)(s nnndsl w.f-. .h.== sss@%^ ~ jddk lXafn^ Dadnd.

EP1: Ding here. Okay, still a load of nonsense I'm afraid. We're now six minutes from passing each other. Again please use you name to start your message. Ding. Over.

EP2: Dan% skrc c*&3 aldm og&n eyx(al@s sk:e f5nf nd,s eepp wtga rbl% 3sks ld4. Dan^ O%%3

EP1: Ding still here. Am I guessing right that you're getting garbled message too? And perhaps you're the science leader Dang Xii? Why are our messages being garbled. I've turned off encryption. I'm going to fire retros to slow down are you going to do the same? Ding. Over

EP2: Dang 45$ a8c fk) lsm (9: edr kd+ dcx q@[{ l qre ier rwo u)e ett mp* nwl 67w eno w$$ Dan 6. O43r.

EP1: Ding here. Beginning to get somewhere, Dang. We're about 3 minutes to close encounter. Ding. Over.

EP2: Dang Ur ((((p an dd dd && fn lo ee am de ee   de to n) l e en ex I4 n) 2. 2m 9$ $. Le ft sd ee ie !! !! Da ng Ov er.

EP1: Ding here: My computer is using an algorithm to unscramble your messages. It says the blast on the mothership must have fried both of our antennae electronics and says you are warning me? Really? Have I offended you? Oh, and we should both head ninety degrees to port to be far from each other at 2.2 minutes. Explain please. We might better survive if together. Ding Over.

EP2: D a n g ! ! ! N u k s s e n g @ n e u n s r t a a a b l e d k g t a s w a I I I d k d l w o e g e t a w a y. D a n g Over.

EP1: Ding My computer says you have an unstable nuclear engine. It says for you to disengage it while you continue to fire impulse jets to slow yourself as we are. Ding Over.

173

EP2: Dang: You are idiot. But at least your words are now making sense. I can't turn off my engine. We cannot veer off at right angles. Why not? Do you know what a "preprogrammed escape pod" means? My computer is intermittently offline. Dang Over.

EP1: Ding Yay we're talking. Your speech was garbled before. My computer is attempting to handshake yours using CNSA override protocol. It might take another 1.7 minutes. Ding Over.

EP2: Dang No time you fool. Our combined speeds still too fast for linking. Try to reach orbit at 94km above ground level, attempt to override the preprogram and try again. If you don't we'll be close enough to collide next orbit. Dang Over.

EP1: Ding. I'm all for that but we'd need to be going in the same direction to link or come to a near dead halt. I think I'll try and contact SpaceWeb before trying to override anything. Ding Over.

EP2: Dang You'5 brea& ngut anda nimbe cile. We'cep a$$d eacho other Foel watsp ends x3&*2l eerts. D&ng Obaa.

EP1: Ding I got most of that, I think. Yes we've passed each other and so stop decelerating cos it's using precious hydrazine fuel for manoeuvring jets. Over.

EP2:   D@ng:bVd8n7FoFGN0eNxcvvny qZD@H16   PGS$k ZmmfA+mw X8G Ms9Z xcmtDQ mAZFdwcD&ngOvrr

EP1: Ding. It's no use Dang, you're probably not getting coherent messages from me either. Next time we pass each other --- let's see in 65 minutes time, we'll be closer and make some sense of each other. Ding Over.

EP2:
Damg*P=D3GkY#q&FzdFxCGRRRR2AYuONCR
ETINCRETINCRETIN&Cb@Qs5z

D   I   N G D ANGDING D A N
G D   I   N   G

E ND

Dedicated to Mark Iles, writer of SF and former Leading Radio Operator in the Royal Navy including during the Falklands conflict.

Meet The Authors

Carl Hughes

Carl is a writer and journalist who has worked for the national and provincial press in the UK and has had his articles published worldwide, from the UK to Australia, India to the US. His fiction has appeared in many anthologies and magazines and he has won numerous writing competitions. He specialises in writing about the offbeat and bizarre, with a special love of horror and Twilight Zone-type stories. He is married and lives in Norfolk with wife Linda.

Chris Rodriguez

Chris Rodriguez has retired from the horrors of conventional life. She now lives on the brink of inspiration in a 100-year-old cottage in Pocatello, Idaho. Her works have appeared in print and online in various formats and themed anthologies including Rhetoric Askew, several by Horrified Press/Thirteen O'Clock, Left Hand Publisher's, Mindscapes Unimagined, ParABnormal Magazine, DL Russell's Nobody Goes Out Anymore, Gravestone Press, The Writer's Prison's Second-Hand Creeps and Blunder Woman Productions, Wrong Turn, which has recently won Best Audiobook Anthology at the SOVAS Awards.

Geoff Nelder

Geoff Nelder lives in Manchester with his physicist wife, cycling rural lanes for thinking time.

Geoff is a former teacher, now an editor, writer and fiction competition judge. His novels include historical fantasy Vengeance Island; Scifi: Alien Exit; The ARIA trilogy; The vegan scifi Flying Crooked series with Suppose We released 2019 followed by Falling Up; Kepler's Son expected out late 2021
thrillers: Escaping Reality, and Hot Air.

Collections: Incremental– 25 surreal tales more mental than incremental.

Ian McKinley

Ian McKinley is a Scot, living in Switzerland and spending much of his time in Japan. A professional scientist and fan of all forms of science fiction in books, comics and movies, he decided at the turn of the century to extend from writing text books and technical papers to the new challenges of fiction. Writing occurs mainly during long vacations spent diving, skiing and exploring exotic locations, which provide inspiration and settings for his books.

He writes novels set in the middle of this century, major social and environmental changes along with rapidly developing technology forming the backdrop for action thrillers written for a mature audience. The characters play a central role, tacitly establishing the cultural changes resulting from increasing sexual permissiveness and growth in the power of mega-corporations at the expense of national governments. As Ian has a wide overview of the most recent developments in science and technology, the future worlds described are credible and, given their generally dystopic nature, maybe worryingly so.

Jackk N. Killington

Jackk N. Killington lives in Missouri where he writes stories and Novels when he isn't working and helping his roommate. Jackk has been published in multiple mediums branching from Webzines to Anthologies and magazines.

Liam A Spinage

Liam A Spinage is a writer, former philosophy student, former archaeology educator and former police clerk. He lives next to a graveyard on top of a hill overlooking the sea, which should be quite enough adventure for anyone.

Marise Morland

I've always been a science fiction fan, and I've had SF and fantasy stories published in various magazines since the 1980's. I'm also a published poet. From 1988 I co-produced a comic strip "Time and Ms. Jones"; which was serialised in the Sunday Times and recently reprinted in Italy. I have just completed a series of space opera novels which are now on sale at Fiction4all.com, and other platforms.

Rickey Rivers Jr.
Rickey Rivers Jr was born and raised in Alabama. He is a Best of the Net nominated writer and cancer survivor. His work has appeared in the JJ Outre Review, Stellium Literary Magazine and Fabula Argentea (among other publications).

Rie Sheridan Rose
Rie Sheridan Rose multitasks. A lot. Her short stories appear in numerous anthologies, including Killing It Softly Vol. 1& 2, Hides the Dark Tower, Dark Divinations, and On Fire. She has authored twelve novels, six poetry chapbooks, and lyrics for dozens of songs. She is also editor-in-chief for Mocha Memoirs Press and previously served as editor for the Thirteen O'Clock imprint of Horrified Press. She is on X and BlueSky as @RieSheridanRose.

Wynelda Ann Deaver
Wynelda loves finding fantastical stories in everyday life. She can often be found with a mug of hot coffee with either a book in hand or one of her own stories flowing from her pen.